"Most women want the richest man around!"

Abby's denial was prompt and emphatic. "That's not true!"

"Isn't it?" Giles asked. "Then why are you here? Or do you expect me to believe you really enjoy the prospect of living with and working for a woman in her mid-seventies!"

"That's exactly what I prefer," Abby cried. "Living in a nunnery would be a pleasure compared with living with you."

"Is that so?" With startling suddenness his mouth came down on hers. She struggled to free herself but she was like a sparrow trying to free itself from an eagle, and he merely held her more tightly, forcing her lips apart by the pressure of his own.

Never had she imagined that she would find herself halfway across the world from home—in the arms of a man like Giles!

Other titles by

RACHEL LINDSAY
IN HARLEQUIN PRESENTS

Other titles by

RACHEL LINDSAY
IN HARLEQUIN ROMANCES

RACHEL LINDSAY

man of ice

Harlequin Books

TORONTO•LONDON•NEW YORK•AMSTERDAM
SYDNEY•HAMBURG•PARIS•STOCKHOLM

Harlequin Presents edition published May 1980
ISBN 0-373-10359-X

Original Hardcover edition published in 1980
by Mills & Boon Limited

CHAPTER ONE

ABIGAIL WEST looked at the cheque for one thousand pounds and debated what she should do with this unexpected windfall. It was not a serious debate, for deep in her heart she knew exactly what she was going to do.

Common sense told her to put it in the bank for a rainy day, but the streak of devil-may-care she had inherited from her grandmother—whose Christian name she bore—told her quite firmly to do nothing of the sort. No indeed; she was going to spend it. Every single pound. And not on anything sensible like a new wardrobe or clothes, which she badly needed, or a moped that would do away with strap-hanging in the subway during the rush hour, but on a glorious, wildly extravagant holiday to the one country she had always wanted to visit : India, land of the Moghul Kings whose stories she knew by heart. India, whose curry she assiduously cooked for herself twice a month; whose paintings she enjoyed seeing, whose music she enjoyed hearing and whose wise gurus she painstakingly tried to understand.

Folding the cheque, she put it in her handbag and sent up a heartfelt prayer of thanks to the electronic calculator that had chosen her name as one of the winners of a Premium Bond.

'You're crazy to spend the entire amount on a holiday,' her friend Millicent Thomas protested later that day when Abigail told her what she was going to do. 'Why not bank half of it? That will still leave you with plenty to spend.'

'Not enough for me to get to India. The cheapest holiday I can book is nine hundred and fifty pounds. That will give me fifty pounds to spend on clothes.'

'At least you'll have something over,' Milly grumbled. 'As for the rest.... Once a holiday has ended, you've got nothing to show for it.'

'That won't be true of this holiday,' Abby replied. 'I'll have thousands of memories to cherish for the rest of my life.'

'Memories!' Milly scoffed. 'That's all you live on. If you don't wake up and start to live in the present, you'll end up an old maid. If you want to use your money for a holiday, why not go to the Bahamas or the South of France?'

'I'd just as soon stay at home as do that. Oh, Milly, can't you try to understand the way I feel? Ever since I can remember I've wanted to go to India.'

Milly pulled a face. 'It would do you more good to go to America—I still can't fathom why you let your mother and sisters go to California without you.'

'Because I didn't want to emigrate, that's why. Anyway, when Mother and the twins went, it was the best thing that happened to me.'

'You're only saying that because——'

'I mean it,' Abby interrupted her friend. 'You can't imagine what it was like to be the ugly duckling in a family of three swans. My mother is as beautiful as my sisters,' she added.

'You've never admitted that before.'

'It's only recently that I've admitted it to myself. I used to feel so awful for being envious of them. If they'd been selfish or conceited it would have made things so much easier for me. But they were always so loving—and that made it worse. They would have been horrified if they'd guessed how I felt. They can't help being breathtaking to look at, any more than I can help being plain.'

'You aren't plain,' Milly said staunchly. 'You're small and slight, but there's nothing wrong with you that new clothes and proper make-up couldn't put right. And that's what you should spend your money on, Abby, not this crazy Indian trip.'

'Crazy or not, I'm going!'

'Why not write to your mother and see what she says?'

'I don't need to write. I know exactly what she'd say —the same as you.' Abby's small triangular face became unexpectedly serious. 'She's a great believer in putting things aside for a rainy day; probably because my father did the exact opposite, and when he died, she was left with debts, a hefty mortgage and the twins and myself to bring up. She wouldn't go out to work and leave us, so she took in lodgers and cleaned and cooked herself into exhaustion.'

'Still, things worked out fine in the end. It was fantastic the way your sisters won that beauty competition.'

Abby nodded. 'They were wonderful to us. The minute they started earning big money, they took over the running of the house and all the money problems.'

'There aren't any problems when you've got money,' Milly said sarcastically. 'And I don't see why you should be so grateful for what they did for you. Damn it, you acted as their unpaid maid and hairdresser for years. The more I think of it, the more convinced I am you should have gone with them to the States. You might have found fame and fortune for yourself.'

Abby laughed. 'Now who's living in dreamland? No, Milly, I'm much better off here. It's marvellous not to be compared with the fabulous West twins and not to have your boy-friends meet them and immediately forget all about you.'

'What boy-friends?' Milly asked bluntly. 'Whenever anyone asks you for a date, you say no.'

'Only because I haven't liked them.'

'How can you tell until you go out with them? Or are you waiting for Prince Charming to come along and sweep you off your feet?'

Abby chuckled. 'How clever of you to guess.'

'Well, you won't find him in India.'

'Perhaps I'll never find him. That's why I want to spend this money in one wildly extravagant way.'

'Well, at least you're spending the money on yourself and not on one of your lame ducks.'

'Now you're giving me a guilt complex!' The words were accompanied by a half joking expression, but Abby meant what she had said. 'Mrs Perkins needs a new wheelchair and . . .'

'Don't you dare! If she moaned to her doctor the way she does to you, he'd see she got one. No, Abby, if you're going to blow that win, then blow it on yourself.'

Three days later Abby did exactly that; signing a cheque for nine hundred and fifty pounds in favour of Gallway and King, specialists in Indian holidays.

'It's a decision you won't regret,' the tour operator said as he handed her a receipt. 'Three years ago I went on the same tour and it's the experience of a lifetime.'

Feeling as if she were floating on air, Abby left the office. There were six weeks to go before the great day, and she knew she would count every hour of them.

*

Driving in the Gallway and King coach to Heathrow Airport, Abby had to pinch herself to make sure she was not dreaming. Eight other people were travelling with her, and they were all middle-aged and looked affluent; the men in well cut tweeds and the women in suits and furs.

Abby wished she were wearing something nicer than her serviceable grey wool dress and jacket, but with only fifty pounds to spend on clothes she had concentrated on summer ones, knowing that once she reached Delhi she would put her winter things behind her. It was scaring to realise she was going to spend Christmas among strangers in a strange land, while her own family was thousands of miles away from her. But at least she would be in the sunshine too, which was a cheering thought.

She frowned, knowing she was verging on self-pity. Had she remained in England she could have stayed with Milly and her parents in Devon, or have spent her time with Mrs Perkins, the old lady who lived on the ground floor of her lodging house. But instead she would be eating her Christmas meal in Bombay— curry and rice in place of turkey and chestnut stuffing.

She grinned at the thought and a dimple came and went in her cheek. It was a softly rounded one, warmed by a flush of excitement which also gave sparkle to her pansy brown eyes. They were her loveliest feature: large, innocent eyes whose corners tilting slightly upwards gave her a faintly exotic appearance. Yet in all other respects she was like an English elf: five feet nothing of skin and bone, her mother had once affectionately described her, and Abby had regretfully known it was true. Not quite so apt now, perhaps, for gentle curves had replaced the angles, but, compared with her glamorous sisters, she was still remarkably unremarkable. She glanced down at her hands. Fine-boned as the rest of her, they were clasping a leather-bound copy of the *Vedac*, a book of ancient Indian theology which had been a holiday present from Mr Rogerson, whose small antiquarian bookshop she helped to run.

Unable to go to university—for though a grant would have kept her there, it would not have helped her to contribute financially to her mother who was still struggling to bring up fourteen-year-old twins—Abby had regretfully had to decline further education and find herself a job. The one with Mr Rogerson had been an unexpected stroke of luck, put her way by her head-mistress, whose distant cousin he was.

'He's an antiquarian in every sense of the word,' Miss Williams had explained. 'He has this wonderful bookshop but stubbornly refuses to engage an assistant; consequently the place has become more and more of a muddle.'

'What makes you think he'll engage me?' Abby had asked.

'Because you love books and you have a gentle manner.' Miss Williams' compliment had been as rare as it was gratifying. 'You're also intelligent enough to learn quickly. Go and see him, Abby. If you don't like him, there'll be nothing lost.'

But Abby had liked Mr Rogerson very much, and a week later she had become his assistant—though hindrance would have been a better word, she had often thought during the first few months of her apprenticeship, for there was so much to learn from him and so much ignorance on her part to overcome. Yet within six months she was able to cope with many of the enquiries that came in from all over the world, and though she knew she would never be as knowledgeable about old books as her employer, she did at least know what he had in his vast and valuable stock.

A year after her coming to work for him, he had paid for her to take a secretarial course so that she could deal more efficiently with the correspondence, and being Abby, she had graduated in half the time, the top of her class.

'If only the twins were as clever as you!' her mother had sighed.

'They're so beautiful they don't need to be clever,' Abby had replied staunchly, little knowing that in a matter of months her sisters would win a beauty competition that they had entered in a spurt of devilry, and be sent on the first step of their meteoric rise to fame and fortune.

It was a fortune they had generously shared, even offering to pay for Abby to go to university and take her longed-for degree in English. But by then Abby had grown to love her unworldly and absent-minded old employer, and she had refused the chance, though she was grateful not to have to contribute any longer to the family's finances. It had enabled her to start saving part of her salary, and when her mother and the twins had eventually announced their departure for America, she had sufficient money of her own to pay for and furnish a small flat in a not too run-down part of Victoria.

However, her propensity for finding and helping lame ducks made it difficult for her bank account to grow again, or her wardrobe to be replenished, a fact which her friend Milly deplored as much as she did Abby's job.

'When you come back from India, I'm going to make

you look for something else,' she had declared a few nights before Abby's departure. 'If you go on working for that octogenarian you'll end up like him! You should be in a big firm where you have a chance of meeting lots of people.'

'Lots of men, you mean,' Abby had replied, and had then told Milly that her fears for the future were unlikely to be fulfilled, for Mr Rogerson had told her only today that his shop was being pulled down for redevelopment, and that though he would be receiving compensation, he felt himself too old to begin again.

'Not that you need to worry about finding yourself another job when you get back,' he had said. 'My stock and clients will be taken over by Markhams'—he had named another illustrious firm—'and they've said they'll be delighted to take you on as well.'

'You won't go, will you?' Milly had cut through Abby's explanation. 'Now's your chance to get out and do something more exciting.'

'I know. And you're right. But I don't intend to give it any more thought till I come back from my holiday. I'm not going to let *anything* spoil this trip for me.'

Abby thought of this now, as the coach trundled steadily along the motorway, and wondered whether Mr Rogerson's enforced retirement was not another pointer from Fate, indicating that she should follow her mother and sisters to California. She shook her head, only realising she had done so when she felt the gold slide she wore slip down on to her neck. Quickly she caught it and put it into her bag. Her long straight hair was so silky that most slides had a habit of falling off, and the gesture with which she now pushed a honey brown strand from her face was an automatic one and unconsciously graceful.

To distract herself from thoughts that could spoil her holiday mood, she opened her holdall and took out the itinerary. It was already dog-eared from long studying, but she read it again, revelling in the pleasure it gave her to mutter the unusual names : Agra, Varanese, Jaipur ...

She was so absorbed that she only realised they had reached the airport when the coach stopped, and she followed her fellow travellers to the check-in counter.

There was a crowd of people around it and she knew it would be at least fifteen minutes before she was cleared for her flight. Patiently she waited in the queue, watched bright-eyed little Indian children clinging to their mothers' sides while harassed fathers pressed forward inch by inch to have their tickets stamped.

At last she was able to check in, and after watching her large suitcase trundle along the rollers and disappear from sight, she stepped back from the counter, apologising as she inadvertently knocked against a hard, unyielding barrier.

She turned and saw it was the grey-suited arm of a tall, spare-framed man. His height was the first thing she noticed about him; that, and the clear gold of his eyes, which were the most unusual colour she had seen. They were like pieces of amber, and glowed with the same intensity. But his expression was stern, almost forbidding, until he gave a slight smile which immediately softened it. Not that it could ever be described as a kind face, but it no longer looked disdainful as he murmured an apology for being in her way.

'It was my fault,' she said, and gave him a wide smile which instantly froze his own, for as she watched him, his mouth set in an uncompromising straight line and he backed away from her and turned to speak to the tall, angular woman who was with him.

Mother and son, Abby thought, or perhaps grandson, for the woman seemed too old to be his mother. But there was a similarity about them that spoke of a blood relationship; it was seen in the same well-carved features and austere profiles, and they both had distinct lines down either side of the mouth. They gave character to the woman, but in the man they looked harsh. Definitely his grandmother, Abby concluded, but then had to amend the opinion, for the woman put her left hand on his arm and she saw that it was ringless.

Aware that she was staring, Abby left the queue and searched above her head for a signpost that would lead her towards Immigration. She had only gone a few steps when someone touched her shoulder none too gently. She turned and saw the man she had knocked against. But this time he was extending her holdall.

'You forgot this,' he said without a smile, and before she could thank him, he turned his back on her.

What a disagreeable man, Abby decided, and then dismissed him from her mind as she pushed her way through the crowd. Once in the departure lounge, she availed herself of the free sandwiches and coffee, for she had been too excited to bother with breakfast, then wandered over to the bookstall, where she was soon so absorbed that she was surprised when her flight was called on the tannoy.

Stepping on to the blue carpet in the aircraft—so large that it was more like a ship than a plane—Abby already felt herself to be in India as she was greeted by a dusky-skinned air hostess in a purple and turquoise sari. Another air hostess, in turquoise and pink, led her to her seat, which was close to one of the serving galleys and gave her more leg room—since there were no seats in front of it—as well as an excellent view of the cabin decor. No utilitarian scheme here, but highly decorated wallpaper depicting dancing girls, whose robes matched the blue and green material that covered the aircraft seats.

The look of delight on her face must have given her away, for the woman who had come to sit beside her said:

'Enjoy the beauty, my dear, because I assure you the efficiency doesn't match it.'

Abby turned and recognised the woman as the one she had seen talking to the stern-faced man at the check-in counter. She wondered where he was and why the two were not sitting together, but had her answer the moment the woman spoke again.

'You are on the Gallway and King tour, aren't you? You bumped into my nephew at the ticket counter. He was coming to see me off.'

'There was such a crush there,' Abby explained, 'that I think I bumped into everybody!'

'There's always a crush at airports these days. At one time when you flew you were treated with respect. Now you are treated like so much cattle.'

'I'm afraid I haven't flown sufficiently to notice,' Abby smiled.

'Well, I have, and you can take my word for it. We're just treated like animals. If there are delays you're never told why. If there are strikes you're always in the middle of them, and when you do finally arrive at your destination you have to wait hours for the luggage or stand in a queue for security checks.'

'Yet *you* are still flying,' Abby said, the dimple coming and going in her cheek.

'Only for the speed, my dear, not for the pleasure.'
The woman had settled herself more comfortably in
the seat.

'Would you like to sit by the window?' Abby asked,
feeling that the age of her companion warranted the
question.

'No, thank you. I don't like looking out of the plane.'

'Are you nervous?' Abby asked sympathetically.

'Petrified,' said the woman in such a firm voice that
Abby did not believe her. Not only did she sound a
seasoned traveller but she looked it. Her tall, angular
frame was encased in a well-worn tweed suit, with a
surprisingly fine lace-edged blouse visible beneath the
jacket. Her face was a mass of hair-thin wrinkles, apart
from the predominant lines that ran down either side
of her nose, but the features were as strong as they
must have been in her youth and her eyes were still
dark and lustrous though her hair was white. Only her
hands, gnarled and veined, gave away the fact that she
was somewhere in her seventies. Nonetheless she
exuded vitality, and was undoubtedly an intrepid old
lady with an interesting life behind her.

All around them the seats were filling up, and the
aircraft taxied slowly to the runway. The warning to
fasten seat belts and stop smoking was given and as
effortlessly as a bird the jet lifted into the air. With
breathtaking speed the ground dropped away beneath
them. Almost at once the earth was no longer dis-
cernible as the aircraft ploughed through into clouds
and then climbed steadily until it reached the limitless
blue of space. Only then did Abby lean back in her
seat and expel her breath with joy.

Her holiday had begun.

CHAPTER TWO

ALTHOUGH a seasoned traveller would have considered the twelve thousand miles trip to Delhi to have been uneventful, to Abby it was a source of new experiences, each one pleasurable. The huge plane descended at Paris, Geneva, and Beirut, discarding some fifteen per cent of its passengers at the last port of call but taking on an equal amount. During the first two stops Abby had remained on the aircraft, but at Beirut she got off, too excited to sleep, though the old lady beside her had been lost to the world for several hours.

But Abby was determined to savour every moment of her precious holiday, and she wandered round the airport, bright and glittering even though it was the early hours of the morning, and treated herself to a cup of coffee and a sticky concoction of raisins and dates before returning to the plane, where she watched fascinated, as closed trolleys looking like sealed aluminium cases were fork-lifted up and then wheeled into the galley kitchens as their empty counterparts were fork-lifted down and wheeled away. Catering for such a vast number of people caused a good many problems and she marvelled that it was all done with such speed and efficiency.

She took her seat again and then watched as they swiftly rose into the dark starry sky, winging their way on the last lap of their journey.

'Haven't you slept at all?' Her companion's voice brought Abby round to face her.

'I've been too excited to sleep.'

'You'll be tired when you get to Delhi.' Dark eyes surveyed her. 'Well, perhaps you won't. You're young and resilient. It's only old people who need to conserve their energy.'

'Is this your first trip to India?' Abby asked.

'I was here many years ago before she had her Independence, so in a way, you could say it is my first trip.'

'Surely not? The people might have changed, but all the things one comes to see are the same.'

'It depends what you've come to see,' was the dry answer. 'I travel primarily to see people; you are obviously travelling to see *things*.'

Abby nodded. 'Ever since I was a child I've adored all things Indian—their paintings, their statues, their architecture.'

'Then you will be following the whole itinerary?'

'Yes. Are you?'

'I hope so, yes. But it will depend how I feel. Giles— my nephew—was very much against the trip. He thinks I'm too old to be gadding around the world, and if one takes age as a criterion, then he's right.'

'Whether or not you travel should depend on how you feel,' Abby replied. 'Not on how old you are.'

'Well, I feel like a spring chicken and I have more energy than people half my age.'

Hearing the vibrancy in the firm voice, Abby could well believe it. This was no old lady ready to sit by her fireside with cat and budgerigar, but a woman of spirit. It was obvious her nephew did not realise it.

'Do you come from London?' she asked.

'From Hampshire. You are from London, I take it?'

'Yes. I live in Victoria.'

By skilful questioning, Abby was soon disclosing

everything about herself; her job—and loss of it—with Mr Rogerson, and the financial windfall that had brought her on this journey.

'A friend of mine wanted me to spend the money glamorising myself,' she added artlessly, 'but years of living with Belinda and Diana has helped me to accept my plainness.'

'Your sisters must be exceptionally beautiful if you consider yourself plain. With those pansy brown eyes of yours and your——' The woman stopped. 'There's no point in my elaborating. Confidence in yourself must come from within, not from what other people tell you. How old are you, child?'

'Not such a child,' Abby grinned. 'I'm twenty-four. I look younger because I'm small and thin.'

'Tiny and slender,' came the reply. 'Doesn't that description sound much better?'

'Of course. But it's too flattering.'

'On the contrary, I've merely stated what I see. Now tell me your first name. You're far too young for me to go on calling you Miss West.'

'My name is Abigail, but everyone calls me Abby.'

'I'm Matilda Bateman and I'm delighted that we're travelling together. It's a pity we didn't talk to you at the airport. I'm sure Giles would have been much more satisfied if he'd known I was travelling with such a delightful companion.'

Remembering the unfriendly way he had regarded her, Abby did not agree with this assumption, but refrained from saying so.

'It will be interesting to see India through your innocent eyes,' Miss Bateman continued. 'It's so long since I made my first long trip that I can't even remember it.'

'I'll never forget *my* first,' Abby chuckled. 'It will

also be my last. Next year it's Bournemouth for *me*!'

'Such pessimism in one so young! If you want something in life you must always believe you can get it. Providing one has one's health, there are three d's I refuse to accept: despair, depression and destiny. The first two one must always fight against and the last one we make for ourselves.'

The woman's life had obviously led her to believe what she was saying, but it was not a philosophy with which Abby concurred. Destiny was a potent force in which she implicitly believed. Tactfully she changed the subject, and they chatted idly until Miss Bateman fell asleep again. Abby dozed too, awakening only as the stewardesses came round to take away cups and plates and the plane began its descent.

Like an albatross the huge jet landed on the runway, and within minutes passengers were filing out. It was only after disembarkation and Customs clearance that Abby had her first glimpse of the entire Gallway and King contingent. There were twenty in all, and though she was not the only one travelling alone she was clearly the youngest. There were two middle-aged men and a couple of doughty-looking women who she guessed to be civil servants or schoolteachers. The others were married couples in their middle years.

A plump Indian introduced himself as a representative of the company and led them to the small coach that would take them into the city.

'Mr Shiran, your tour guard, will be meeting you all later this afternoon,' he said, 'but for the moment I will deal with any enquiries you may have. As you know, you have the rest of this day free.'

'I want to go shopping,' one of the women said. 'I haven't come all this way to waste a day doing nothing.'

Abby let the conversation wash over her and gazed intently on the passing scene. They were driving through the countryside and for as far as the eye could see the land was flat. It also seemed quite fertile and was divided into surprisingly small fields, no bigger than English ones. But there were very few people to be seen working in them, though occasionally she glimpsed a pair of buffaloes pulling a plough or a woman bent double over the earth. They did not pass through any villages, but now and again she glimpsed small huddles of huts, some of mud and some of straw, which seemed to be bulging with goats and chickens as well as people.

As they approached the city there was no appreciable difference in the landscape, or the road, for though it widened, there were no pavements, merely a slight difference in the texture of the earth where the pedestrians walked. Frequently the coach was slowed down by cows wandering in its path. This was Abby's first glimpse of the sacred beast, though she was to see many hundreds more before her journey was over; poor homeless animals wandering the streets in search of food. Sacred and untouchable, they were left alone to fend for themselves and to die, when they would then be taken away on carts by the city's refuse men. It was an aspect of India she would grow to hate.

At last the coach stopped at the plate glass entrance to the Oberoi Hotel and three-quarters of the passengers alighted, including Miss Bateman. The remaining ones travelled on with her to the less distinguished Noranda Hotel, and only then did Abby realise that most of the group were travelling de luxe. She was too happy at the whole prospect of her holiday to let it worry her, and though she found her room

spartan, it was clean and had a functional bathroom
with plenty of hot water.

The dining-room was modest and though the chairs
were hard and the tables wooden ones, without benefit
of cloth, the lunch she was served was wholly Indian
and excellent: a delicious mutton curry with freshly
ground spices, their flavours mingling yet each subtly
retaining its own.

Lunch over, Abby unpacked half of her suitcases,
then, unwilling to remain indoors, made up her mind
to do a little exploration of her own. One could not fly
halfway around the world and then immediately go to
bed. Changing into a sweater and skirt, though she
was still not sure how warm it was, and carrying a
cardigan under her arm, she left the hotel and wandered through the streets.

The first thing that struck her was the absence of
traffic, and what there was of it was old-fashioned and
ramshackle, with small military jeeps outnumbering the
old Morrises and Austins. Of bikes there was a plethora,
for this seemed to be the main transportation apart from
the infrequent single-decker buses, so full of humanity
that they would have made a can of sardines look
empty. The shops she passed were small single rooms,
some were two-storied and most of them served also
as home for the merchants who squatted cross-legged
inside them, surrounded by their wares. And what
wares they were! Trinkets and silver, glass and copper
and metalware, spice shops filled with jars, their coloured interiors making them glitter like jewels. Leather-
work painted, stitched or plain, and an eye-catching
display of sari lengths in silk and cotton, all glowing
with colour.

Afraid to wander too far from the hotel, she paused

to look more closely at some of the jewellery, delighted by the skilled workmanship and amazed at the cheapness. But she had vowed not to buy anything too soon, and she resisted the blandishments of the merchants who called to her and proffered their wares. As she paused to look at some things, several beggars approached her: two boys not yet in their teens, their scraggy bodies clad in tatters but their eyes shining with mischief; a dark-skinned woman with sagging breasts and a child sucking one of them, and a little girl in a filthy dress with a face like an angel. But they all had one thing in common: outheld hands and the plea for money. It was one that Abby could not resist, and digging into her purse she took out all the loose coins she had and distributed them. Almost simultaneously she felt as though a thousand vultures were descending on her, as the pleading beggars disgorged themselves from heaven knew where and flung themselves upon her, voices raised, hands outstretched.

'Baksheesh! Baksheesh!'

'I've got no more,' she cried. 'I've given you all my change. Please let me go.'

As she went to move, more beggars descended upon her, and her gentle efforts to break free met with such failure that she began to push harder. Only by pushing at full strength was she finally able to make a path for herself. Hands to her ears to obliterate their cries, she ran for dear life, pursued by several of the more hardy ones who did not give up the chase until she stumbled through the fly-spotted door of her hotel.

Never had she thought to be so pleased to enter its dingy interior or to find the smile of its brown-skinned proprietor so warm and welcoming. A glance through the glass door told him swiftly what had happened and he came round the reception desk with a look of concern.

'It's best that you do not give money to beggars,' he said in a lilting sing-song voice. 'Otherwise they will never leave you alone and one will become a hundred.'

'I know,' she said. 'But it's so hard to refuse. One of them was only a little girl.'

'You must harden your heart,' he replied. 'The Government keeps saying they will bring out legislation to stop begging, and it will be a good thing when they do.'

Abby could not see anything commendable in stopping them; it was necessary to stop them from *having* to beg. But that was so vast a problem that India could not deal with it alone.

She went towards the stairs and her foot was on the first step when the proprietor came hurrying over to her, a slip of paper in his hand.

'There was a call for you,' he said. 'Miss Bateman would like you to have dinner with her at the Oberoi. If you wish, I will get you a rickshaw taxi. It is too far for you to walk.'

'Are taxis expensive?' she asked.

He looked surprised. 'Everything is cheap for the tourist here. For twenty pence you may go anywhere in Delhi. But it is wise to arrange the price before you start the journey.'

A little later, sitting on the hard, narrow seat of the basketlike contraption that was perched on a three-wheeler bicycle, with her driver furiously pedalling, Abby came to the conclusion that it was worth spending a few rupees more to sit in a taxi proper, in comfort, which was not a way that this journey could ever be described. Nor did she enjoy being pulled along by another human being.

But the man was delighted with the money she gave him when they reached the Oberoi, and offered to wait and take her back.

'I'm having dinner here,' she said. 'I'll probably be several hours.'

'I wait. If I get another job, I come back later. But you please wait for me.'

'No,' Abby said firmly. 'I won't wait for you and I don't want you to wait for me either.'

Before he could argue, she entered the lobby, where Miss Bateman, resplendent in vintage black moiré, greeted her warmly.

'I'm so delighted you came, child. I hadn't realised we weren't staying in the same hotel. Is yours comfortable?'

'Yes, thank you. And the lunch I had there was delicious.'

'I hope you're not too full to enjoy dinner. The restaurant here is supposed to be one of the best in the city.'

'I'm never too full to eat,' Abby confessed.

Miss Bateman laughed and led her into a Moghul-style dining room where for the next few moments they gave themselves over to the serious business of choosing their food. Once it had been ordered, the older woman began to talk about India; its architecture and literature; its food, religions, and the different traditions of the various cultures.

It was a wrench for Abby to leave, but she was unwilling to let Miss Bateman tire herself, and noting the flush on the lined cheeks, she regretfully pushed back her chair.

'If you don't find me an old bore,' Miss Bateman said briskly, as she accompanied Abby through the lobby, 'I would be happy to have your company during the tour. Unless of course you meet someone of your own age.'

'I shouldn't think that likely. They're all very old on this tour.'

Abby caught her lip, annoyed by her lack of tact. But Miss Bateman chuckled.

'It's only the middle-aged who object to being called old. When you reach my age, you take it as a compliment.' A gnarled hand patted Abby's arm. 'What I really meant to say is that if you do share your time with me, you must never have any hesitation in telling me if you wish to spend your time with someone else.'

Promising she would remember this, Abby returned to her hotel. The small room was welcoming and she had no sense of loneliness as she undressed and climbed into bed. It was hard to believe she was actually in India. Smiling, she closed her eyes and was instantly asleep.

At seven next morning she awoke to a hazy grey sky. Hurriedly she showered and dressed. There was a morning of sightseeing ahead and the coach was calling here at eight-thirty before going on to the Oberoi to collect the rest of the group; travelling de luxe also gave them half an hour longer to lie in.

Although there were many historic monuments to see, for the average sightseer there were only a few of interest. The most important was the Red Fort, an excellent example of Moghul architecture that Abby had assiduously read about before coming here.

Yet she was unprepared for the splendid sight of thousands of small green parrots nesting on the vast sandstone walls, which gave the Fort its name. The main entrance ran through a covered passage that teemed with shops selling tourist trivia, but since most of it was glittering and cheap it beguiled the eye.

'We will stop here on the way out, if you wish to buy anything,' the guide informed them. He was a well-spoken man in a shabby suit, who rattled through his information like a gramophone record that had been played too many times.

Abby would have preferred a more leisurely inspection of the Red Fort, for she was anxious to savour all she was seeing, and though she tried to keep up with the group, she soon found herself lagging behind and, on her own, wandered across the spacious lawn that led to the Great Hall.

It was an awe-inspiring sight, even though most of the inlaid precious stones had been prized from the walls by British soldiers after the Indian Mutiny. It was here that the Crown Moghul had held public audience, though it was in the smaller Hall of Private Audience that Abby saw where the famous Peacock Throne had once stood, before being taken to Persia. Originally the ceiling of this marble room had been fashioned from solid silver, and there were still many fragments to be seen, as well as some wonderful Florentine panels. But it all had a faded glory that was vaguely depressing, and it was not until she reached the Royal Harem and baths that she felt she had walked straight into a page from the Arabian Nights.

It was difficult to believe that this huge edifice had offered shelter against the extremes of the Delhi climate, where the winter nights and mornings were cold, and where the summer temperatures reached a hundred degrees in the shade. Yet man's ingenuity had cooled the heat with intricate water channels, and kept out the cold with marble screens and curtains of heavy gold and silver brocades.

Abby was still musing on what it must have been like

to live here when the Red Fort was occupied, when she heard her name called by the guide and saw him march over to find her.

'You must please stay with the party,' he said irritably. 'Otherwise you will get lost.'

'But I like to look at things more slowly and to study the guide book. . . .'

'Then you should come back here again on your own. You have another day of leisure tomorrow.'

She nodded dutifully and followed him to where the rest of the group were waiting.

'I'm going to come back later with another guide,' Miss Bateman informed her as they continued on their way. 'I shall be more than happy for you to join me.'

'I'd love to,' Abby said. 'But only if you let me pay my share.'

'Don't be silly, child. It will be a pleasure for me to have your company.' They walked towards the coach. 'If it weren't for my nephew I'd be staying at your hotel. But he insisted I pay due regard to my age and travel first class once I got here.'

Abby tactfully made no comment. Her curiosity about her companion had grown rather than diminished, for there were certain discrepancies in the woman's behaviour that she found intriguing.

Miss Bateman stayed at the Oberoi, yet she wore clothes that had been in their heyday thirty years ago, and though her handbag was a crocodile one, it was so worn that some of its skin had been rubbed away. Had she once been rich and come down in the world, or had she always been poor and relied on wealthy relations like her nephew to take care of her? Somehow she did not strike Abby as being the sort of woman who would continually accept charity, no matter with what love it was dispensed.

'It's such a pity Giles wouldn't come on this trip,' the old lady broke into Abby's thoughts. 'But he says he's seen as much of India as he wants.'

'I can't imagine him coming on a tour like this,' Abby replied with more truth than tact. 'He doesn't look the type to be hassled by a guide.'

'He isn't.' Miss Bateman chuckled at the mere idea. 'But Giles has never been here as a tourist. He came to work.'

'To work?'

'Yes. He's still here, in fact. He was only in London for a few days to see one of the Ministers. But he's lived in India for the past three years. He's in Bombay now, but for two years he travelled extensively in the Northern States. He's one of the top men in nuclear engineering. At the moment he's supervising the building of a nuclear reactor.'

Abby looked suitably impressed as Miss Bateman continued to expound on her nephew's brilliance. There was no doubt now in Abby's mind that he was paying for his aunt's trip, for the woman had also disclosed that he had been orphaned at thirteen, from which time she had taken care of him.

'I knew nothing of children and cared for them even less,' she went on, 'but having Giles in my home opened up a new world for me. He was an adorable child.'

Abby tried, but failed, to visualise the forbidding-looking man she encountered at Heathrow airport as an adorable child.

'But even as a child he was incredibly gifted.' Miss Bateman was still in full flood of reminiscence. 'He was always mischievous and unexpected and loved trying to hoodwink you. I remember in his first year at Eton he fell from a tree and got concussion, and when he woke up he pretended he couldn't speak English. For a whole week he fooled everyone by talking Latin!'

Abby swallowed hard. The interest that Giles of the amber eyes had inspired in her at their first meeting turned into awe. It was a good thing he had not accompanied his aunt on this trip after all. What sort of conversation would interest and amuse a man who, at fourteen, had spoken such fluent Latin that he could trick his masters for a week?

'I'll be seeing Giles in Bombay, of course,' Miss Bateman said. 'The tour group will only be there for four days, but I'm planning to spend a month with him. Maybe longer, if I feel I need it.'

'Need it?'

'Need the rest,' Miss Bateman said quickly, and gave Abby a sidelong glance that made the girl wonder if the words had held any other significance.

'Is your nephew married?' she asked.

'Only to his job. I often tell him that one day I expect him to make me godmother to a newborn power station!'

Abby giggled. It might never be possible for her to laugh with the erudite Giles, but listening to Miss Bateman's teasing references to her nephew, it was certainly possible to laugh *at* him.

CHAPTER THREE

DESPITE being so talkative about her favourite relation, Miss Bateman gave away nothing of herself, and Abby knew no more of the old lady's past than she had first done.

One thing only was clear: that she adored her nephew and that he was extremely fond of her. But then she was an easy woman of whom to be fond, for she was intelligent, humorous and, despite her occasionally abrupt manner, kindly. She did much to make Abby's stay in Delhi enjoyable, insisting that she keep her company each evening and taking her by private taxi to the places they had seen earlier in the day. She never allowed Abby to pay any part of the expense, and Abby concluded that it was all being borne by the generous Giles.

By the time they reached the Clark–Shiraz at Agra, travelling to it in an air-conditioned coach, the group had already settled into little cliques.

'It beats me why half of them have come on this tour,' Miss Bateman remarked on their first afternoon in the city. 'For most of them it's only a shopping expedition with all the magnificent buildings thrown in as an optional extra.'

'I don't blame them for buying things. Some of the jewellery and brocades are lovely.'

'I haven't noticed you succumbing.'

'I wouldn't have use for such things. I don't lead that sort of life.'

'Then you should, a pretty girl like you.'

Abby shook her head, then pushed back a strand of honey-gold hair. 'The one thing I'm not is pretty. Intelligent, quick-witted, bright—I'll allow you almost any adjective except the one you've just used.'

'Then you're neither intelligent nor bright,' Miss Bateman retorted. 'Not if you can say a thing like that. You *are* pretty, my dear.' Eyes that were incongruously bright in the lined face surveyed Abby with embarrassing thoroughness. 'Perhaps pretty is the wrong word for you. Elusively lovely is a much better description.'

Abby was too amused to be embarrassed, and seeing it, Miss Bateman gave an irritable snort.

'What do you call lovely?' she demanded. 'Having a big bosom and silver-blonde hair?'

'Not really.' Abby gave the question a little thought. 'But it's certainly important to have a good figure.'

'What's wrong with yours?'

'I'm too small. No five-footer has ever won a beauty contest.'

'Don't set your standards by today's mediocre one,' Miss Bateman snapped. 'Big is not always beautiful. I suppose it was your two selfish sisters who robbed you of your confidence?'

'The twins weren't selfish.' Abby's response was immediate. 'And I'm not lacking in confidence.'

'Perhaps not on the intellectual level. But on the emotional one you are still a child.'

'My sisters can't be blamed for that.'

'*I* blame them,' Miss Bateman said. 'They should have taken you in hand.'

'They did try,' Abby replied. 'But their idea of glamorising me wasn't mine. I'm not the type for false eyelashes and sexy clothes, and when they saw how silly I looked in them, they—they——'

'They gave up and left you alone?'

'They were very busy with their careers,' Abby said defensively.

Miss Bateman's reply was forestalled by their being called to take their places in one of the taxis waiting to take the group on their first visit to the Taj Mahal.

'Tomorrow we will see it by daylight,' their guide informed them. 'But for the first view of the Taj, there is nothing more beautiful than to see it in the moonlight.'

His words were prophetic. Abby, walking through the tall main gate and having her first glimpse of this marble monument to love, knew she would never see anything more heart-catching for the rest of her life. A thin mist was rising from the river that lay behind the Taj, and it drifted in soft wisps around it, so that one could almost believe the building was floating on a timeless sea. The sky above was dark and the full moon hidden by clouds which cast their shadows across the perfect dome, making the whole building seem to rise like some gigantic airship ready to take to the sky.

'Let us go closer,' the guide suggested, and led the way down the long garden, past the narrow rectangular pool that reflected the Taj in every aspect of its continually changing moods.

They passed the entrance to the Tomb and stared at the ninety-foot-high archway that led into it, before moving to the east side where they perched on a marble wall and let their gaze rest on the slender marble minarets that marked the four corners of the Tomb. It was difficult to believe that man could have dreamed, let alone constructed, an image of such magnificence, and Abby felt humbled as she thought of the twenty thousand slaves who had worked and died here in order

to give marble form to a Moghul Emperor's tribute to
a dead wife.

As she went on staring at the Taj, all the facts she
had read about it became unimportant. It did not
matter that it was a tomb of love nor that it had taken
twenty years to build. Everything that had gone into
the making of this most perfect of all creations became
insignificant in the sight of the creation itself.

I am here and now, the Taj seemed to proclaim.
What has gone and what will be doesn't matter. I am
of no time and place. I am you!

Momentarily she turned her eyes away from the
sight of so much beauty. The Taj was everything she
had expected and nothing she had expected. The emotion she felt was too deep to be put into words. How
could one describe colour to a man who had been blind
from birth, or a chord of music to someone born deaf?

Slowly everyone in their group started to wander
away; some to take other vantage points, some to move
closer to the monument. But Abby and her elderly companion remained seated on the wall, letting themselves
experience without thought. It needed no words to tell
Abby that the woman felt exactly the way she did, and
it increased the empathy she already felt with her. A
sigh escaped her and, hearing it, Miss Bateman gave
her a sharp glance.

'No tears, Abby.'

'It's too beautiful for tears.'

'The Emperor turned his tears into marble and built
this tomb. He thought of nothing else for the rest of his
life.'

Abby sighed again. 'He must have loved her very
much to have wanted to give her such a resting place.'

'Basically, it's the sort of thing I abhor.'

'You don't like the Taj?' Abby was flabbergasted.

'No, no, I didn't mean that. How could I? But building a shrine to love is a dissipation of energy and emotion. No matter how deeply you love someone, you should accept their death and go on living. One must look forward, not back.' Miss Bateman sneezed and pulled her coat more closely around her. 'I suppose you think I'm a prosaic old woman?'

'Not at all.'

'Well, I am.' Another sneeze brought Miss Bateman to her feet. 'It's chilly here. I think I'll take a taxi back to the hotel. But don't come with me,' she said as Abby went to rise. 'I'll see you tomorrow. We've a long day of sightseeing ahead.'

It was not an overstatement. For hour after hour they were all enthralled by the sights and sounds of Agra; a street market, where one of the women in the party had her bag stolen; a temple—as crowded and noisy as the market had been—where they listened to a priest wailing in prayer, and the Taj Mahal in daylight, as exquisite as it had been in the silver light of the moon.

Dusk was already falling as they returned to the Clark Shiraz where, after dinner, a display of Indian dancing was being held in the hotel garden.

'Not for me,' Miss Bateman said to Abby. 'I'm feeling tired, and dinner in bed will do me more good.'

Abby looked at her carefully and saw a marked flush on the sallow skin. She was glad they were all staying at the same hotel for this part of the tour, and after she had had dinner she went up to Miss Bateman's room to see how she was.

In a thin cotton nightdress with ruffles at the neck and wrists, the woman looked far more her years than in her usual old-fashioned silk suits. Her voice was husky and in the middle of greeting Abby she went into a fit of coughing which momentarily left her too exhausted to speak.

'Don't you think you should see a doctor?' Abby suggested.

'Whatever for? I'm prone to bronchitis and anything sets it off. It's my own fault for sitting on that marble wall at the Taj last night.'

'Do you have any medicine with you?'

'I took some a little while ago, but you may fetch me my cough mixture from the bathroom.'

Abby did so, taken aback by the number of medicine bottles arrayed round the sink. If Miss Bateman needed all this, it was no wonder her nephew had been apprehensive at her travelling alone.

'I don't think I'll do any sightseeing tomorrow either,' the old lady stated after another bout of coughing. 'I visited Fathepur-Sikri the last time I was here, and I'm sure it hasn't changed.'

'It's supposed to be a marvellously preserved city.'

'But a dead one, like Pompeii. Four hundred years ago it was the principal residence of the Moghul court, but after Akbar died—he was one of their greatest emperors—it fell quickly from favour. Still, it's worth seeing.'

'Everything in India is worth seeing,' Abby said so fervently that Miss Bateman laughed.

'You make me realise how wonderful it is to be young.'

'It's equally wonderful to be young in heart the way you are.'

'Thank you, my dear. That was a lovely thing to say. Come in to see me as soon as you get back tomorrow.'

Long before the time of departure next morning, Abby was waiting impatiently for the mini-bus. Yet conscience would not let her board it until she had made sure Miss Bateman was all right, and she raced up to the woman's room.

Her first sight of the old lady told her that the woman was suffering from more than a cold. Her face was puffy and her eyes bright with fever. She also seemed to find it difficult to concentrate for long, and in the middle of telling Abby not to miss the coach, she started to mumble incoherently. It was then that Abby knew it was time to call a doctor.

The desk clerk told her that one was already in the hotel visiting another guest, and that he should be available within the next half hour.

'Your tour guide is waiting for you,' the man added. 'Please hurry.'

'He'll have to go without me,' Abby replied, battling against her deep disappointment. 'I wouldn't feel happy to leave Miss Bateman alone.'

'We can arrange for a maid to sit with her.'

The temptation to agree was strong, but conscience would not let her, and Abby thanked him and refused the offer.

Within a few moments of the tour departing, the doctor arrived. He was middle-aged and plump, and his body was encased in a tight-fitting Indian-style jacket that buttoned high at the throat.

His examination of his patient, who was almost comatose, was thorough, and his expression so serious as he did so that Abby feared the worst.

'It's a severe bronchial chill,' he pronounced finally. 'I will give you some antibiotics, but I don't expect any favourable result for twenty-four hours.'

'Do you think she should go to hospital?' Abby asked.

'Not yet. I won't decide finally until I see her later today. In the meantime I will arrange for the medicines to be delivered to you.' Black eyes raked her face. 'You are a relative?'

'A friend. But I'll be staying with her all day.'

Nodding his satisfaction, the doctor left, and Abby settled in a chair by the bed, book in hand. At least she could read about the ancient stone city whose visit she had missed.

The doctor returned later in the afternoon, by which time Abby could see for herself that Miss Bateman's condition had worsened. Her breathing was difficult and she rambled on about people and places Abby did not know, or else lay quietly, except for stertorous breathing.

'There's no need for alarm,' the doctor assured her. 'By the morning there should be some improvement.'

Abby was not quite so sanguine about this, and her fears increased as the evening progressed, strengthening when Miss Bateman once again began to ramble in delirium.

'Stop bullying me, Giles! I'm not a child. I've travelled around the world twice before you were born, and I've no intention of spending the remainder of my life in a wheelchair. I may be old, but I'm neither senile nor in poor health.'

Abby smiled. Delirious or not, Miss Bateman sounded exactly the way she always did. How angry her nephew must have been! Even though she had only had a brief glimpse of him at Heathrow airport, she had known he was not a man who liked to be overruled. There had been a noticeable air of command about him, and the little she had learned of him from his aunt had only served to reinforce her first impression.

Abby moved quietly over to the bed. Miss Bateman seemed to have shrunk and, for the first time, gave the impression that she might not recover. If this were so, how would her nephew react at not having been told his aunt was ill, particularly when he was already in India?

After a moment's hesitation, for it was difficult to make herself search through someone else's belonging's, Abby opened Miss Bateman's handbag on the dressing-table and searched in it for a diary or address book.

Luck was with her, for in a calf notebook she found several names and addresses, including that of Giles Farrow in Bombay.

At once she put in a call, and spent the time waiting for it by nervously pacing the room, one moment convinced she was doing the right thing, the next chiding herself for being unduly hysterical. Then the telephone buzzed and there was no time for any more fears, for Miss Bateman's nephew was on the line, his voice sounding sharper now that it was disembodied.

'You don't know me,' she began swiftly, 'but I'm travelling on the tour with your aunt. You—er—I bumped into you at Heathrow and——'

'What's wrong with my aunt?' He interrupted her abruptly and, annoyed with herself for having gone into an unnecessary explanation—what did it matter to him who she was or whether or not they had met?— Abby quickly told him of his aunt's condition.

'The doctor says there's nothing to worry about, but . . .'

'But you're worried enough to ring me.'

'Yes,' Abby said firmly. 'I wouldn't have done if we'd been in England, but . . .'

'I'll get the first plane I can. I doubt if I'll be able to

make it tonight, but I should be there some time in the morning.'

She was surprised by the swiftness of his decision.

'I wasn't expecting you to fly up here, Mr Farrow,' she said.

'Why did you call me, then?'

'To put you in the picture. But if——'

'Well, now you've done so, kindly leave the decision to me.'

With a crisp goodbye he hung up, and Abby put down the receiver, relief mingling with irritation. What an annoying man he was! Yet she was glad she had called him, for she no longer felt she was carrying the entire burden of Miss Bateman's illness. If anything happened to the woman between tonight and tomorrow, when her nephew arrived, nobody would blame her for not having done her best.

Picking up the telephone again, she asked to have dinner served in the room, then went over to the window and stared wistfully into the gloom. It had been a tedious and dispiriting day. Sitting for so many hours watching someone in a state of unconsciousness was no way to spend a holiday.

She yawned and stretched, suddenly anxious to have Giles Farrow here to take command of the situation. What a relief it would be to give up all her responsibility!

With a sigh she sat beside the window and cupped her face in her hands. The view was beautiful, with the Taj a pale glimmer in the distance. But somehow the scene was dominated by the memory of amber eyes, whose gleaming warmth was in such contrast to the crisp, cold voice.

CHAPTER FOUR

ABBY slept surprisingly well in the armchair beside Miss Bateman's bed, and did not awaken until the lightening of the sky heralded a new day.

Instantly she sat up straight and looked at the bed. Miss Bateman was still asleep, but her face was not so flushed and her breathing was less rasping.

Abby frowned. Had she waited until this morning before calling Giles Farrow, she would have had second thoughts. But it was too late to think of that now. If the man was to be taken at his word, he was already winging his way here from Bombay.

A glance at her watch told her it was past seven and, careful not to make a noise, she went into the bathroom to shower. She felt much better after it, even though she had to put on the same clothes she had worn the day before. She thought longingly of the crisp cottons hanging up in her wardrobe but was reluctant to return to her room and leave Miss Bateman alone. When she returned to the bedroom, Miss Bateman was already awake and regarded Abby with astonishment.

'Good gracious, child, what are you doing here?'

'I stayed with you last night.'

'With *me*? You mean you didn't go back to your own room?'

'The doctor didn't want you to be left on your own. But I slept perfectly well here—the armchair was extremely comfortable. Now how about my ordering some breakfast? What would you like?'

'Some tea but nothing to eat.' The dark brown eyes narrowed. 'I can't remember much about yesterday. I know you came here in the morning, but after that it's all somewhat vague. Was I off my head?' she demanded with characteristic bluntness.

'Teetering on the brink,' Abby smiled, and wondered whether now was the time to announce the impending arrival of Giles Farrow. Drawing a deep breath she did so, her misgiving fully justified as Miss Bateman gave an angry snort.

'It was very naughty of you to call him. He's extremely busy and dislikes being bothered.'

'He didn't sound to me as if he disliked it. He said he was very glad I called him.'

'Of course he'd be glad—Giles and I are very fond of each other. But he's still too busy to come all the way here when it isn't necessary.'

'When I telephoned him last night I thought it was very necessary. You seemed awfully ill and I was worried. Perhaps if we'd been in England with English doctors I might have felt differently.'

'There's nothing the matter with Indian doctors. You must learn not to be so insular, child. You're too intelligent.'

'And too untravelled,' Abby said ruefully, accepting the criticism. 'But all things being equal, I'm not sorry I contacted your nephew.'

'Did he say what time he would arrive?'

'This morning. But he didn't give an exact time.'

Noon came and went without Giles Farrow's arrival and his aunt decided he had caught a mid-morning plane. As the day dragged on Abby's regret at having called him decreased, for Miss Bateman's earlier show of improvement vanished and her temperature rose again. She remained mentally alert, however, though unusually quiet and content to doze.

It was only when they had both had lunch, Miss Bateman managing to swallow some soup and a small portion of plain cooked rice, that she seemed to realise how much sightseeing Abby had missed, and became so distraught by it that the flush on her cheeks intensified.

'You won't get another chance to see Fathepur-Sikri. If you didn't want to leave me yesterday, you should at least have gone there today. It was stupid of me not to have hired a car and a guide to take you there.'

'I saw the Taj Mahal,' Abby said stoutly. 'That made up for everything.'

Miss Bateman looked unconvinced but did not argue. 'What time is the group leaving for Jaipur?'

'We have to be at the airport by six. That means leaving here at five. But *you* won't be coming.'

'I realise that. I may be an obstinate old woman, but I'm not gaga enough to think I can get out of bed and go on a long flight.' Miss Bateman struggled into a sitting position. 'You'd better go to your room and pack. You don't want to be late.'

'It won't take me long to get ready. I didn't unpack properly in the first place. If I leave you when your nephew arrives, I'll still have loads of time.'

But Abby's intention showed no sign of being carried out, for at four o'clock there was still no sign of Giles Farrow. Miss Bateman had fallen asleep again, after a heavy bout of coughing, and Abby was loath to waken her. She glanced at the telephone, then tiptoed from the room and made her way down to the reception desk, where she asked one of the clerks to call the airport and find out when the next plane was due in from Bombay.

'There are only two direct flights today,' the man said. 'One arrived at eleven this morning and the other was due in at two but has been delayed by engine trouble. It may arrive later today or not until to-morrow.'

Dismayed, she stared at him. 'I know Mr Farrow wants to get here as quickly as possible. I'm sure he'll try to get on another airline.'

'No other airline operates internally in India—only our State-controlled one.'

Biting her lip, Abby went in search of the Gallway and King courier. As she had expected, he was outside the hotel talking to a few members of the group who, cases already packed for departure, were watching an Indian snake charmer. Abby looked at the huge snake writhing on the ground and hastily averted her eyes.

'Mr Shiran!' she called, and the man turned and came towards her.

'And how are you today, Miss West?' he said with polite punctiliousness. 'It was good of you to spend all your time with Miss Bateman. She is lucky to have such a valued friend.'

Abby ignored the fulsome compliment. 'Is there any change in the time of our departure?'

'No. We leave at five o'clock as arranged. If your case is ready, I will have it brought down.'

'I haven't packed yet. You see Mr Farrow hasn't arrived.'

Seeing the Indian's perplexity she hurriedly explained who Mr Farrow was, and that he was probably booked on the delayed flight from Bombay.

'But I can't leave Miss Bateman until he gets here,' she added.

'Why not? Doctor Bira is the best medical man in Agra, and if necessary he will send her to a hospital or private clinic.'

'I still can't leave her until I'm positive Mr Farrow is on his way.'

'Why don't you telephone his home and find out? Someone is certain to know what plane he caught.'

Annoyed with herself for not thinking of this—her brains must have gone into cold storage for the holiday—Abby rushed back into the lobby and made the call from a downstairs telephone. It took her more than a quarter of an hour to get through, and she fumed with impatience. But this was India—where modern technology went hand in hand with inefficiency, and she controlled her temper and waited.

Finally her call came through, and she returned to Mr Shiran with a frown marking her forehead.

'Mr Farrow has definitely left Bombay,' she said. 'His housekeeper told me that he had to see some Minister in a town en route. But she doesn't know where. That means he must be catching another flight from a different place.' She flung out her hands. 'It's no use—I'll have to stay. Perhaps you can get me on a plane for Jaipur tomorrow?'

'I doubt it. These flights are booked weeks ahead. But of course I will try,' he said soothingly, and motioned Abby to accompany him to the reception desk while he did so.

'The news is not good,' he said, swinging round to her. 'You are wait-listed on tomorrow's flight, but you are number fifteen in the queue.'

'What will happen if I don't get on?'

'Your name will be transferred to the flight for the day after. But by then we will be on our way to Udaipur, so you will have to get yourself a different reservation. And there may be a delay there too.' He frowned. 'I think it best to book you directly to Udaipur.'

Abby nodded and tried to look pleased when Mr Shiran finally informed her that he had managed it. It meant she would miss Jaipur, which she had been very keen to see, as well as having missed most of the itinerary for Agra.

Swallowing her disappointment, she watched as the other members of the tour boarded the coach which was to take them to the airport. Watching it disappear in a cloud of red dust she felt unexpectedly homesick. Although she had not been on more than nodding terms with any of her fellow travellers it was disconcerting to know she was now left alone to fend for herself. No, that wasn't true. She still had Miss Bateman.

Pushing her self-pity aside, she went to her room at the rear of the hotel and changed into another dress before making her way to Miss Bateman's far larger one overlooking the gardens and a distant view of the Taj. Her elderly friend was sleeping and she tiptoed over to the armchair and sat down.

From somewhere in the distance came the monotonous twanging of a sitar. It was curiously restful and helped to soothe her jangled nerves. Her disappointment lessened and became a dull ache in the recesses of her mind. What did seeing a few ruins or a town or two matter when compared with giving comfort to another human being?

Comforted by the question, she closed her eyes and relaxed.

The sudden switching on of the light startled her into wakefulness, and she sat up straight.

Giles Farrow was in the room: tall, rangy and looking ridiculously English with his proud carriage and haughty face. Before either of them could say a word, Miss Bateman raised herself in the bed and beamed at him with a mixture of delight and shame.

'Giles my dear, I'm so sorry to have brought you all this way for nothing. I'm *much* better now. Abby should never have called you last night.'

'Last night you were ill,' he replied, and strode over to the bed. With surprising gentleness he bent and pressed his cheek to the lined one. 'Don't apologise because you're better. I'm delighted by it.'

'Even though you've had a wasted journey? Oh, Giles, I'm so sorry.'

'The journey was worth it—if only to have you apologise twice in one minute! I can't remember you ever doing that.'

Miss Bateman tossed her head, but before she could make a rejoinder she broke into a paroxysm of coughing which kept her nephew by her side, watchful and attentive as he handed her a tissue and then, as the coughing subsided, pouring her some fruit juice. Only when she had taken a few sips did the old lady look across at Abby with a tender smile.

'And now, my dear, I'm delighted to say that I'm off your hands.' She glanced at her nephew. 'This poor child missed the whole tour yesterday and another one today.' She looked at Abby again. 'But at least you won't be missing any more, so run along with you and enjoy your stay in Jaipur. But leave me your address in London so that I can contact you there. I've something in mind which I would like to talk over with you.'

Abby rose to her feet. A surreptitious glance at her watch showed her that by now the tour was already winging its way to Jaipur. She was aware of Giles

Farrow looking at her in a coldly critical way, and wondered what she had done to merit it. Was he, despite
what he had said to his aunt, annoyed with her for having brought him from Bombay on an unnecessary
journey? Her own irritation with the man gave her the
impetus to speak.

'I'm afraid the group has already gone, Miss Bateman. They left at five o'clock, and it's now eight.'

Astonishment and then contrition flashed across the
classical features that not even age could destroy. 'My
poor child, why on earth didn't you tell me? You knew
Giles was coming. You should have left!'

'Mr Farrow's plane was delayed,' Abby said, not
looking at him. 'And ... and no one knew quite what
time he would be arriving.'

'That was still no reason for you to have stayed
behind.'

'I wouldn't have been happy to have left you alone.
Honestly, I didn't mind. It gives me an extra day here
and I—and I can go to Fathepur-Sikri tomorrow. That
way I won't have missed it.'

'What a good idea. Then you will leave tomorrow
evening for Jaipur?'

Abby's hesitation only lasted for a split second, but it
was still long enough for Miss Bateman to look at her
with shrewd eyes.

'You've missed the Jaipur trip too, haven't you?'

'Yes. Mr Shiran couldn't get me on a flight out of
here until the day after tomorrow.' Abby made her
voice bright. 'But there wasn't all that much to see at
Jaipur, and I'll use the time here to go to the Taj again.'

'It's monstrous that you've missed so much of your
tour,' Miss Bateman protested, and looked at her
nephew. 'We must think of something, Giles.'

'For the moment I'm too tired to think of anything,' he said abruptly. 'I've had one hell of a journey here and right now I'd like to bathe, change and have dinner.'

'Then go and have your bath and then take this poor child to dinner with you. I absolutely insist that she doesn't stay in my room any longer.'

Abby felt the amber-gold eyes survey her.

'I'll meet you in the Moghul Room in an hour,' came the clipped words.

She nodded, though had it not been for Miss Bateman she would have refused such an ungracious invitation. Indeed in fairness one could not call it an invitation, for he had been bludgeoned into it by his aunt.

'In an hour,' he repeated, and strode out.

Alone with Miss Bateman, Abby debated whether to say she did not wish to dine with Giles Farrow, then decided to hold her tongue; but she was hardly looking forward to a meal with her tongue.

'I don't know how to thank you for staying with me,' Miss Bateman murmured. 'You have a truly generous heart.'

'Anyone else in my position would have done the same,' Abby protested.

'No, they wouldn't. They might have stayed for an hour or possibly an evening, but then they'd have handed me over to a nurse—which is what you should have done. No, my child, you *do* have a generous heart.'

The words brought tears to Abby's eyes and she blinked them away, knowing they showed that self-pity was still too close for comfort.

'I'll go to my room and change,' she said huskily, seeing it as an excuse to avoid any further thanks.

'Good. My nephew hates to be kept waiting. It's the only time he's inclined to lose his temper.'

Biting back a sarcastic comment, Abby smiled and went out.

CHAPTER FIVE

ARRIVING at the top floor of the hotel a few moments before the hour was up, she found her host already waiting. He had changed into a beige linen suit with a matching silk shirt. In the dim pink light his hair looked darker, though nothing could disguise its mahogany tinge as he seated himself opposite her at a side table.

'You have the choice of Indian or European food,' he said tersely.

'I always have Indian,' she replied. 'I'm horrified when I read stories of people travelling round the world having bacon and eggs for breakfast and roast beef for dinner. One might just as well stay at home.'

'It depends on the state of one's stomach. If one is used to a specific diet it's best to stick to it.'

Faced with such logic she subsided into silence, wishing she had had the courage to refuse his invitation, regardless of what his aunt might have said. Resolutely she studied the menu. Many of the dishes had unfamiliar names, and though in normal circumstances she would have had no hesitation in asking the waiter to tell her what they were, under the aloof eye of Giles Farrow she played safe and said she would have Tandoori chicken.

'What else with it?' her host asked.

'Is it necessary to have anything else with it?'

'If you're hungry, it is.'

'I'm starving,' she confessed. 'I only had a snack at lunch.'

'Too busy playing the ministering angel?'

There was no mistaking the sneer in his voice and she longed to get up and leave the table. But with an effort she controlled herself.

'I'm glad you're hungry now,' he went on. 'Is it because you've got what you wanted?'

'I beg your pardon?'

'You've brought yourself to my aunt's attention. That's what you wanted, wasn't it?'

Abby was not sure she had heard correctly, but the anger on Giles Farrow's face told her she had not misunderstood the implication behind his words. For a reason best known to himself, he thought she was deliberately trying to get round his aunt.

'I don't know why you have such a bad impression of me, Mr Farrow.' Abby found her voice was trembling and she stopped and waited for it to steady itself before continuing. 'But I can assure you it was quite a sacrifice for me to remain with your aunt and lose part of my tour. I can't afford to come to India again, and this trip means a great deal to me.'

'Not as much as my *aunt* could mean to you. You could have many interesting trips with her if you continue to play your cards right.'

Angrily Abby faced him across the table. 'What am I supposed to want from your aunt, and why on earth should she bother herself with *me*?'

'Because you could be a secretary-companion for her,' he said bluntly. 'This is the first time she's travelled alone. Until now she's always had someone with her to do her typing and to keep her notes in order. It's an excellent job and I don't blame you for wanting it. Six months in a country mansion and six months travelling all over the world is quite an attraction.'

'I don't know what you're talking about. I had no idea that your aunt employs anyone and——'

'Spare me the pretence. You'll be telling me next you don't know who she is.'

'Is it so important to be your aunt?' Abby asked with sweet sarcasm.

He gave a tight, unamused smile. 'I give you full marks for trying, Miss West, but you damned well know who my aunt is. Everyone's heard of Mattie Bates.'

'Mattie Bates?' Abby echoed. 'You don't ... you don't mean Miss Bateman is ... But I'd—I'd no idea! You do mean Mattie Bates the detective writer, don't you?'

'I do,' he said tersely, 'and please spare me the rest of the act.'

'I'll do better than that, Mr Farrow. I'll spare you having dinner with me.' Furiously she jumped to her feet. 'I've had as much of your insinuations as I can take. Whether you believe me or not, I'd like to get the record straight. I didn't know your aunt was anyone other than a charming old lady travelling on her own. And if you want something else to disbelieve, then I'll tell you that I thought *you* were paying for her holiday!'

Without giving him a chance to reply she swung away from the table and walked blindly towards the door.

She was standing by the lift, her fingers pressed on the button, when he caught up with her.

'You're supposed to be having dinner with me,' he said coldly.

'Have it by yourself. I'm sure you'll enjoy it more.'

'I'm sorry if I've made you angry, Miss West.'

'You haven't made me angry. I'm quite used to being accused of making up to old ladies. As a matter of fact I usually insure them for a hundred thousand pounds before I bump them off!'

The lift doors opened and she stepped inside.

'Please come back to the table and talk to me,' he said quickly.

'No, thank you, I'm going to bed.'

The doors closed and only as the lift descended did she lean against the wall, aware that she was shaking as though with fever. What an unbelievably hateful man he was, and how distorted a view he must have of people if he believed she had befriended his aunt in order to better herself.

Mattie Bates. The name brought to her mind much of what Abby had read of the creator of the fabulously successful Mr Gill and Alphonse Drake, those two masterminds of detective fiction who had headed the best-seller lists since their creation thirty years ago. And it was not only with books that Mattie Bates had found fame, but also with the plays and films that had been made highly successfully from them. Her wealth was legendary and she used it to obtain the maximum privacy for herself.

The lift doors parted and Abby stepped into the foyer. It was obvious that Giles Farrow had a deep sense of guilt at being the beneficiary of so much wealth: a guilt that made him suspicious of anyone who tried to befriend his aunt. The thought increased her dislike of him and, in an effort to forget the whole unpleasant scene that had just taken place, she decided to treat herself to a rickshaw drive.

She crossed the lobby and paused beside the revolving doors.

'You wish for taxi car?' the night porter asked.

She hesitated, then said she wanted a taxi bike, deciding that this would be cheaper.

He hailed one from a long, waiting rank, and she gingerly clambered on to the narrow seat and gave the name of another hotel which she had seen on her drive to the Taj Mahal the first night she had arrived in Agra.

As her driver began to pedal, the cold wind whipped around her, though it did not cool her temper, which bubbled away steadily as she went back over her conversation with Giles Farrow. How dared he accuse her of deliberately making herself indispensable to his aunt? He did not know the woman if he thought her capable of being at the mercy of any young girl with her eye on the main chance. Miss Bateman was an astute judge of character, as her comments about those on the tour had already shown Abby; only in her judgment of her nephew did she seem to be totally wrong.

'I'll leave here first thing in the morning,' Abby muttered aloud. 'And if I can't get a flight out, then I'll move to another hotel. That should show Mr High-and-Mighty that I've got no aims in his aunt's direction!'

Having made this decision, Abby's temper lessened sufficiently for her to take in her surroundings, and she saw the taxi bike had come to halt and that the driver had turned round on the saddle to face her.

'Long way to hotel,' he said. 'You pay ten rupees more.'

Abby was taken aback. Then she became afraid. But she knew she dared not show it, and she looked back at the man with as much haughtiness as she could muster.

'I won't pay you one single rupee more. We've already agreed a price.'

'I change my mind. Is a long far journey. You pay eight rupees instead.'

'No,' Abby repeated. It was not the price which made her reluctant to hand over the money—to a Western pocket it was a ludicrously low sum anyway—but the knowledge that she dared not put herself in the position of being held to blackmail.

'I'll pay you something extra when we get to the hotel,' she said.

'You no pay, I no take you.'

'Then I'll find someone else who will.'

Quickly, before her courage deserted her, Abby jumped to the ground. There were no street lights to guide her, and with only a sickle moon for illumination, she hurried down the road. There were no other vehicles or people in sight, and she was by no means sure she would be able to find another taxi. All she did know was that she was not going to argue with her Indian driver or give in to his demands. To have done so would have encouraged him to ask for more, perhaps even to snatch her purse and kill her. Terrified by the thought, she ran even faster.

'You come back to rickshaw, lady.' A sibilant voice, almost in her ear, told her that the man was keeping steady pace alongside of her. 'Get back in,' he said softly.

'No, thank you, I'm going to find someone else to take me.'

'No one around so late. It is too far for you to walk. You come with me, lady. I no take money now. I wait till we get to hotel.'

'No,' she repeated, and quickened her pace. There

was a look on the man's face she did not like and she
had no intention of getting back into his rickshaw. The
end of the road was only about twenty yards away and
she could dimly discern a large grass-covered round-
about. On it were small mounds of what looked like
bundles of dirty washing, but Abby knew each bundle
was a human being sleeping there for the night because
they had no home to which they could go. She had been
horrified when Mr Shiraz had pointed out these desti-
tutes to them on their first visit to the Taj, but now she
saw them as her only hope of escaping the man beside
her.

'I not want to frighten you, lady. You take seat in
rickshaw and we go to hotel.'

Without replying she tried to quicken her pace. But
there was a stitch in her side and she could not go any
faster. Behind her she heard the rumble of a car, and
its lights picked out the dusty road ahead of her. But
instead of going past, it slowed down and a face peered
out through the window.

'Miss West?'

With a gasp of astonishment she stopped dead and
looked into Giles Farrow's chiselled features.

'Why are you running along the road?' he asked
abruptly.

'The man wanted to be paid in advance and I didn't
think it wise to do so.'

'Neither is it wise for you to be going on foot. Get
in,' he ordered, and opened the door of the taxi for her.

Pride made her want to refuse the offer but fear
impelled her to accept it, and without a word she
clambered into the seat beside him. Only then did he
say something in Indian to the cyclist. Abby did not
understand it, but the tone made translation unneces-

sary, and she was not surprised to see the man pedal away for dear life.

'What did you say to him?' she asked faintly.

'I told him if I saw him hanging around the hotel any more I'd have his hide.'

'How did you know where to find me?' she asked.

'I didn't. It was sheer chance that I took this route. I followed you down to the lobby, but you'd already gone out. The porter told me you'd taken a rickshaw bike and I decided to follow you. Unattached females shouldn't go traipsing across the city at night. And if you did want to, you should have had the sense to take a car.'

'They're more expensive.'

'A few rupees only,' he shrugged. 'I refuse to believe you're that hard up.'

The tone of his voice told her he was serious and she marvelled that he could have so little understanding of the way many people had to live: on a fixed budget where every penny counted.

'I came on this holiday with a specific amount of money to spend,' she said coldly, 'and anything I fritter away means I'll have less left over with which to buy things. A couple of rupees might be unimportant in themselves, but they have the habit of mounting up.'

'I considered you sufficiently intelligent to value your safety more than a few extra rupees with which to buy baubles.'

'Oh, you're impossible!' she snapped, and lapsed into an angry silence.

A few moments later they were back at the Clark Shiraz, and as the taxi drew to a halt she fumbled at the door to get out.

'Just a moment,' said Giles Farrow. 'I think you should know that I've changed your room.'

'You've what!' Astonishment kept her motionless.

'I've asked the hotel to change your room. It was at my aunt's behest, not mine. She wants you to have a room with a view of the Taj.'

Tears came into Abby's eyes and she blinked them away. Dear Miss Bateman! How unlike her autocratic nephew she was.

'That won't be necessary, Mr Farrow,' she said. 'I'm leaving Agra tomorrow and there's no point moving my room for one night.'

'It's already been arranged.'

'Then unarrange it.'

She jumped out of the taxi and ran into the hotel. She was at the reception desk asking for her key when Giles Farrow caught up with her.

'Don't make an unnecessary fuss, Miss West,' he said softly. 'My aunt wishes to show you a kindness in return for your own, and it's petty to refuse.'

She swung round on him, tilting her head up sharply so that she could meet his eyes and wishing she were a head taller. Amber eyes stared back at her, their colour intensifying as he gave a slight, unexpected smile.

'For someone so small, you have a mighty fine temper. But I'm too tired to argue with you any longer. If you don't do as my aunt wishes, I suggest you go up and tell her.'

Abby's small white teeth caught at her lower lip, aware that Giles Farrow had skilfully made her look childish.

'Very well, I'll do as Miss Bateman wants.' She flashed him a bright hard glance. 'Paying for me to have a better room for a night doesn't mean very much to her. She could probably buy the hotel without noticing it!'

For an instant he looked startled, then realised she was being deliberately provoking, and he glanced down at his watch.

'I don't know about you, Miss West, but I'm exceedingly hungry. You made me leave my dinner before I'd even started it and my appetite refuses to be allayed any longer. I intend to continue with my meal and I suggest you retire to your room and do the same.'

Before she could think of a suitable retort, he turned on his heel and strode away, leaving her to cope with an assorted mixture of emotions: anger, amusement, dislike.

But it was amusement that predominated as she was given the key to a bedroom on the same floor as Miss Bateman, and entered it to find her luggage already there, having been packed and unpacked by one of the many young Indian maids who flitted silently about the hotel. It was the most luxurious room she had ever stayed in, and she bounced happily up and down on the bed, then more soberly opened her case and lifted out some of her things. She was too hungry to unpack properly and she was debating what to order when there was a knock at the door and, at her command to enter, a waiter wheeled in a laden trolley.

She looked at him in perplexity. 'I didn't order anything.'

'Order came to kitchen,' he replied, and left the trolley beside the window. 'If you wish for anything else, please call me.' He backed out respectfully, leaving Abby to lift the silver-covered dishes and stare at the steaming hot food: crisply baked chicken, steaming rice mixed with dried fruit and cashew nuts, aromatically spiced spinach.

She knew at once that Giles Farrow had ordered this

for her, and though the thought almost robbed her of her appetite, it did not succeed. Pulling up a chair, she started to tuck into the food. The surroundings were not as glamorous as the Moghul Room, but at least she had no need to make conversation with a man she detested.

Her fork was motionless in the air. Detested was too strong a word. Disliked was a better one. Yes, she definitely disliked Giles Farrow.

CHAPTER SIX

WITH an excellent meal inside her, Abby presented herself at the door of Miss Bateman's room and, seeing a light coming from underneath it, knew the old lady was not asleep.

'How lovely to see you,' Miss Bateman exclaimed, as she went in. 'I'm so glad you had dinner with Giles. It gave you a chance to know each other.'

Abby smiled without answering, unwilling to let the woman know that she and the beloved nephew were as close to knowing each other as a rattlesnake and a rabbit. And I know exactly who's the rabbit, she thought wryly as she perched on the edge of the bed.

'You look heaps better, Miss Bateman,' she said.

'I feel it. You look better too.' Miss Bateman eyed Abby's flushed cheeks, their pink matching the dress whose figure-fitting bodice hugged small curving breasts and a tiny waist. 'Do you like your room?'

'It's lovely. But it was extravagant of you to do it. I was quite comfortable where I was.'

'But now you can see the Taj—which I know you love.'

Their glances met and they smiled, happy together.

'I don't want you to stay up here and keep me company,' Miss Bateman continued. 'I understand there's dancing in one of the rooms downstairs.'

'Pooh to that,' said Abby. 'I can always go dancing in London.'

'Do you?'

'Not often. But that's from choice. I find most men

62

of my age too childish, while the older ones are either married or on the prowl.'

'Looking for bedmates, you mean?' Miss Bateman saw Abby's expression and chuckled. 'I'm not as dated as I look.'

Abby smiled back. 'You must have thought me an awful fool for not knowing who you were. When Mr Farrow told me, I——'

'Giles told you?' His aunt looked annoyed. 'I should have warned him to hold his tongue. I intended telling you myself when we got to Bombay. You see, I've something in mind for you.'

'Really?'

'Can't you guess what it is?'

Abby could, having spoken to Giles Farrow, but she was reluctant to say so. Instead she made a negative sign and waited for the woman to tell her.

As expected, it was an offer to become her secretary companion.

'Don't give your answer now, child. Think about it carefully. My home is in the country and your life with me would be a quiet one. I still travel, of course, and you would accompany me, but I don't go away as frequently as I did, and for eight months of the year you would be isolated. I would also work you hard.'

'Having given me all the reasons why I should refuse your offer,' Abby smiled, 'shouldn't you tell me why I should accept?'

'Because you told me you loved the countryside. Because you're fond of animals and if you lived with me you would be able to have a dog of your own. Because you'd like to travel, and my next trip will be to Jap Miss Bateman paused. 'But I still want you to thin over carefully.'

Abby stared at the carpet. 'Does your nephew come to see you often?'

'He hasn't done for the past three years since he's lived in India. But he's returning to England in a few months, so I daresay he'll come for a weekend every month.'

'Does he know you're offering me this job? He won't approve, you know. He thinks I've been nice to you because I've been angling for it.'

'Which just goes to show that even the cleverest of men are fools when it comes to judging women. No wonder I've never married!' Miss Bateman eyed Abby seriously. 'Don't let Giles upset you. He's always been concerned to see that no one takes advantage of me, and since I know *you* also have my best interests at heart, it should give you something in common.'

Abby bit back the comment that the only thing she and Giles had in common was their antipathy for each other.

'I'd love to work for you, Miss Bateman. It sounds a wonderful job.'

The old lady looked delighted, and Abby forced herself to think of this when she saw Giles Farrow the following morning outside his aunt's bedroom.

'So you got what you've been angling for?' he commented coldly.

'If you say so, Mr Farrow,' she answered demurely. 'I wouldn't dream of trying to change your opinion of me.'

'You wouldn't succeed. You may fool my aunt, but you'll still have me to contend with.'

'Watching to make sure I don't steal the silver?'

'Luckily the bulk of her money is tied up in trusts,'

he replied without expression. 'So nobody can take advantage of her any more.'

'Not even you?'

He took a step in her direction and Abby drew back in alarm. But he was instantly in control of himself, though his eyes were filled with contempt as he opened the door of his aunt's room and let her precede him inside.

Miss Bateman was sitting in an armchair by the window, almost her old self in a faded beige dress and jacket.

'I think I'll go out for a stroll,' she announced, after greeting them. 'But you, my dear Abby, are going to Fathepur-Sikri. I've booked a car with a driver guide to take you there. He's waiting for you downstairs.'

Abby's eyes glowed with pleasure, giving her face a sudden beauty that was quenched the instant she saw the dislike on Giles Farrow's face. How easy it was to guess his thoughts!

'You shouldn't have ordered a private car for me,' she said. 'I'm sure I could have found a group to join.'

'Don't let's discuss it, child. It's all settled. Now go off and enjoy yourself.'

And enjoy herself Abby did. Like the Red Fort in Delhi, the town of Fathepur-Sikri was built of red sandstone. But here all the similarity ended, for the decoration of all the buildings was extremely delicate and the carvings on the stone pillars so perfectly preserved that it was hard to believe they had been done when Shakespeare was a boy.

Though the site was supposed to be a protected area, vandals had already left their mark on it, and several of the walls were marred by ugly graffiti. The thought of it nagged at her during the long drive back to Agra, which partly helped to take her mind off the tediousness of the journey. No one could describe driving by car in India as anything other than a penance, for one had to continuously watch out for pedestrians, who treated road and pavement as if they were one and the same thing, while cows wandered haphazardly betwixt people, bicycles and cars.

Halfway into the city the driver stopped to put some water into the radiator, and the moment he left the car to search for some, it was surrounded by urchins clamouring for money. Even with the windows closed, Abby found the dark intense faces disconcerting. A couple of boys started to bang on the glass, and no matter how fiercely she scowled they took no notice. Luckily no one tried the doors, whose locks were far from secure, though as time passed and more urchins gathered around, they began to press themselves so closely against the bodywork that the car started to shake. Abby felt almost like a film star being surrounded by fans, except that here there was no adulation, only screeching cries for money.

'No mother ... No father ... Money, money ... Ten brothers and sisters ... Money, money.'

Some of the children held up pieces of paper on which was scrawled the miserable story of their lives. Inadvertently, Abby glanced at one through the window pane.

'My mother has no legs and my father is blind. Our home is under a tree.'

With a gasp of horror she closed her eyes and settled back in her seat, praying desperately that the driver would soon return. It was a relief when he finally did, though they had travelled several miles before her body stopped shaking.

'We will soon be coming to another village,' the driver said, half swivelling round. 'Do you wish to stop for some tea or something to eat?'

Hastily she declined, unable to face the prospect of being besieged by beggars again. She was too diplomatic to say so, however, for it almost sounded an indictment of Indian life. It was two o'clock when she returned to the hotel, and after a quick wash she went to the dining-room for lunch. Many of the other groups were still at their tables: a party of thirty Germans, the same of noisy Japanese men, and a quiet group of Scandinavians. Abby was the only one eating alone, and she took the set Indian menu in preference to the European one.

It was only when she was sipping her coffee that she realised she would have to become used to hotel life. Working for Miss Bateman meant she would be doing more travelling than she had dreamed possible. It was hard to assimilate the fact that she had been offered such an opportunity. Living in the Hampshire countryside for nine months of the year might be a disadvantage for many girls of her own age, yet to her it was only a pleasure; one of the many she hoped to gain from her new position.

How much she would be able to learn from Miss Bateman, whose knowledge of life was broad and kindly. It made Abby think of her father, an erudite, gentle man whose death, when she had been a child, had been her greatest loss.

Unseeingly she stared into space, jumping with surprise as Giles Farrow appeared beside her table.

'Must you always act like a startled rabbit when you see me?' he asked with barely concealed irritation.

'I wasn't expecting you.' She avoided his eyes.

'When I saw you this morning I forgot to thank you for having dinner sent to my room last night.'

'I hope the food improved your temper?'

'There's nothing wrong with my temper, Mr Farrow.' She glared at him. 'Did you come in here to find me, or were you just passing through?'

He ignored her sarcasm. 'I came here to tell you that my aunt and I will be leaving for Bombay tomorrow. The doctor has said she's fit enough to travel and I'd like to get her settled in my home.' He paused. 'I know you're planning to go on to Udaipur from here, but when you leave there and come to Bombay, my aunt would like you to stay with us.'

'I would prefer to stay in a hotel. It's included in the price of the tour, anyway.'

'My aunt thinks you would be more comfortable if you stayed with us.'

It seemed rude to refuse; Miss Bateman knew her new secretary-companion did not get on with her nephew, but she would not like to think that the dislike was so active that it would make it difficult for them to maintain the semblance of a relationship.

'Very well,' Abby said. 'I'll try not to be in your way.'

'Just try to be of use to my aunt,' he replied, 'without making use of her.'

Abby caught her breath. Was he never going to drop his antagonism? The question, though unspoken, was obvious enough to make him give her a bleak smile.

'I have a poor opinion of women in general, Miss West, and of young and pretty ones in particular.'

'You can't be referring to me,' she said promptly.

'I didn't think you were the type to fish for compliments.'

'I'm not fishing, Mr Farrow. I just happen to know my limitations.'

'Being plain isn't one of them,' he said stiffly. 'So spare me the pretence.'

Her own anger rose to meet his. Why should he think she was trying to be coy, and what had made him pretend she was anything other than averagely passable?

'There is one more thing I have to say,' he continued. 'My aunt is distressed that you've missed seeing Jaipur, and has asked me to arrange for you to go there.'

'How can I? The tour group will be there today and I couldn't get a flight out in time to meet them. That's why I'm going to go straight to Udaipur.'

'You can go to Jaipur *after* Udaipur, and forget your tour group. I have friends there who will be more than willing to have you stay with them for two or three days, more if you wish it. Then you could join my aunt in Bombay in a week's time.'

It was such a tempting offer that Abby was hard put to refuse, but refuse she must, for she had no intention of being under any obligation to this man.

'I've already paid for two days in Udaipur, Mr Farrow, and I'll be quite content with that. I'll leave Udaipur when the rest of my tour goes, and join your aunt in Bombay afterwards.'

'You're cutting off your nose to spite your face,' he stated.

'Don't let that worry you. It's *my* nose.'

Without a word he walked out, leaving her to sip her coffee, now cold and bitter, and wonder what had happened in his life to have made him the same.

She was unexpectedly given the answer when she joined Miss Bateman by the side of the pool later that afternoon. Giles Farrow was nowhere to be seen and Abby was too grateful for his absence to wonder where he had gone. Not so her companion, who was still fretting at having brought him chasing across the

Indian continent when he still had so much work to do in Bombay.

'One is always extra busy when nearing the end of a project,' she explained, 'particularly one as difficult as this.'

'Has it been a success?' Abby asked.

'Yes indeed. The Indian Government want him to stay another three years, but he won't. He says England needs him more.'

'Then why did he come here in the first place?'

'The Foreign Office asked him to do so. Alliances are built as much on technological exchanges as on commercial ones. It was very difficult for Giles to refuse—especially when the Prime Minister said how important it was.' The woman sighed. 'And of course it cost him his happiness.'

Abby's ears pricked up with curiosity, but she refused to satisfy it.

'Mind you,' her companion went on, 'deep in his heart I don't think he believed Vicky meant what she said. Neither did I really. I thought she was playing hard to get but that eventually her greed would make her give in.'

Abby sniffed. 'I suppose being your nephew has made him very sought after.'

'So has being his father's son. He inherited Farrow Engineering.'

Though she knew little of business, Abby had heard of this one, and realised why her accusation that Giles Farrow was interested in his aunt's money should have enraged him.

'Why are you smiling?' Miss Bateman enquired.

'I was remembering something I'd said to Mr Farrow earlier today.' Abby hesitated. 'We don't get on very well. He distrusts me.'

'He distrusts all women since Vicky let him down. Mind you, even if she had married him I don't think they would have found lasting happiness together. She was always a scheming minx and sooner or later he would have seen her for what she was. Under that tough exterior, Giles is a romantic.'

Abby found this so hard to believe that she did not even attempt it. One could describe Giles Farrow in many ways, but never as a romantic.

'Was she beautiful?' she asked, curiosity getting the better of her.

'Exceedingly so. With very pretty manners and a great deal of charm which she knew how to use. I suppose that's why she expected Giles to do as she wanted. When he didn't, and said he was going to India, she broke off their engagement. Poor Giles, he took it very badly.'

'Why didn't she want to come here? I know Bombay is hot, but——'

'For the first eighteen months of his stay he wasn't going to be in Bombay—except for infrequent visits. Most of that period was going to be spent travelling between Calcutta and Delhi and other northern parts of the country. It wouldn't have been an ideal life for a young bride—I'll admit that—but I'm sure Giles could have worked out something if Vicky had been willing to go with him. But she didn't see herself living in some remote hill station. If she couldn't queen it among the diplomatic circles in Delhi or the rich merchants of Bombay, then she didn't want to come. In the event she married an American millionaire less than two months after breaking off with Giles, and he's remained sour ever since.'

'You think he's still in love with her?'

'If he wasn't, he'd be able to talk about her.'

It was hard for Abby to see Giles Farrow as an un-requited lover nursing a broken heart. But in view of what Miss Bateman had said, there was no other choice. Of course his reaction could be due to hurt pride rather than love. He had such a high opinion of himself that his fiancée's desertion of him must have been deeply shattering.

'What are you thinking about?' Miss Bateman asked. 'You look very sceptical.'

'I was trying to see your nephew through your eyes,' Abby admitted. 'But my own image of him keeps getting in the way. I can see why his experience with his fiancée soured him, but it isn't mature to let yourself become warped simply because of that.'

There was a lengthy silence and Abby was afraid she had been too blunt about her new employer's beloved nephew. She was on the verge of apologising when the woman spoke.

'So you think he's warped, do you? If anyone told him that, he'd say he was only being logical.'

'Warped logic,' Abby said firmly. 'One day he may see it for himself.'

'Only if he falls in love again.'

'I'd like to be around when that happens!'

Miss Bateman smiled. 'I hope you are.'

CHAPTER SEVEN

ABBY had some misgivings about going to Udaipur and leaving Miss Bateman, but contented herself with the knowledge that Giles Farrow—for all his cynicism—was extremely fond of his aunt and would take care of her.

With this in mind she was able to enjoy herself at the old-fashioned hotel that overlooked one of the huge man-made lakes for which the city was renowned. In the centre of the largest of them was the Summer Palace of the Maharajah, now transformed into a hotel. It was here that the de luxe travellers of Gallway and King were staying, but having visited it, Abby was in no way dismayed at being housed in the city itself, where the Winter Palace proved an unending source of delight. It was splendidly decorated with glass and porcelain mosaic, while its museum showed the finest collection of miniature paintings she had ever seen.

The bazaar was also full of interest and she wandered from one tiny shop to another, watching the silversmiths making the intricately designed necklaces and bangles with which Indian women loved to decorate themselves. It was impossible to resist buying a necklace: a delicate filigree affair that winked and glittered as it encircled her neck, and it was so ludicrously cheap that she succumbed and bought a matching bracelet.

Occasionally she thought of Miss Bateman and her nephew, and a glimpse she had of a tall, brown-haired man set her pulses hammering until he turned and she saw he was a stranger. She did not relish the prospect of having to stay in his home in Bombay, but resolutely refused to let it worry her. There was time enough for that when she was there.

Mr Shiran was surprised when she informed him she would not be with the tour once they reached Bombay. He was worried that it was due to something he had done, and she was quick to assure him it had nothing to do with himself or the tour.

'I'm going to work for Miss Bateman,' she explained, 'and it's more convenient if I stay with her.'

'But we will be taking many excursions from Bombay,' Mr Shiraz said. 'Are you going to miss them all?'

'I wasn't booked on any—I couldn't afford them. All I intended to do was to explore Bombay itself.'

'I see. Then in that case you have lost nothing. And I am sure you will find Mr Farrow's home more comfortable than a hotel.'

Abby doubted this, but kept her peace. Not even to herself would she admit quite how nervous she was at having to stay in proximity to such an aloofly disagreeable man.

It was with this thought in mind that she arrived in Bombay at noon the following day, after an uneventful flight across seemingly barren desert. But there was nothing desolate about the swarming airport. People were everywhere, many of them content to sit on the floor regardless of their beautiful saris and well-cut clothes, in order to continue their endless wait for seats on the one and only internal airline.

Giles Farrow had sent a limousine to meet her. The chauffeur was a Sikh and though he wore a grey uniform, he sported a curly black beard and a turban. His foreign appearance left her unprepared for his excellent English and he gave her a running commentary on everything they were passing during their hour-long drive into the city.

Alongside the motorway, concrete blocks of flats, newly erected, already looked like slums, only a little better in appearance than the endless sprawl of shanty towns with their small tin huts that served as homes for entire families. Some of these shanty towns were hidden from sight behind high, ramshackle walls, but for the most part they were on view, and filled Abby with a deep sense of unease. It had been easier to accept such dire poverty in the smaller towns of Northern India, but seeing it here, co-existing with a commercially prosperous business community, it was an appalling indication of man's inhumanity to man.

'Does Mr Farrow live in the city itself?' she asked, forcing her mind away from the heartbreaking sight.

'Yes, lady. He lives on Malibar Hill. That is one of the nicest parts of Bombay.'

Trust Giles Farrow to treat himself to the best! Abby thought critically, and was equally critical of herself for thinking it. Having been told the reason for his churlish manner, she should have sufficient compassion to understand it and sufficient intelligence to ignore it.

'We are nearly there.'

The chauffeur spoke again and she saw they were driving along a tree-lined road with the sea on their right. Bombay was built on several islands linked by causeways, so that one frequently had unexpected glimpses of the shimmering water of the Indian Ocean. The car slowed down as they entered between large wrought iron gates, and swung round a short drive to stop outside a square, three-storied house.

Abby knew without being told that it had once been a palace, and as she climbed the marble steps and entered the large square hall, the splendour of the interior confirmed it. It was like stepping into a Hollywood film set of the 1930s, and she would not have been surprised had an orchestra suddenly begun to play and Ginger Rogers and Fred Astaire danced across the marble floor to greet her.

Instead Giles Farrow walked purposefully towards her, tall and lean, his mahogany brown hair gleaming like satin and his eyes golden as topaz and hard as stone. Her heart hammered in her throat and she had to remind herself that she had no reason to be afraid of him. Yet how hard it was to maintain her composure beneath that cold, indifferent gaze.

'Did you have a good trip?' he asked perfunctorily.

'Yes, thank you.'

'My aunt is in the garden,' he continued, and moved towards the glass doors that lay at the end of the hall.

Abby wished she could go to her room first, to freshen up, but was determined not to ask him. He was such an uncaring man—despite what his aunt said— that he was unable to appreciate how hot and sticky she must feel after her long flight. Easing the collar of her dress away from her perspiration-damp throat, she followed him as he went ahead of her.

He was formally dressed in a pale grey suit and dark tie, and she wondered if he were the sort of man who wore a dinner jacket when he dined alone in the jungle. A dimple came and went in her cheek and she bit her lip to prevent herself from smiling. He opened the glass doors and led the way across a small but lushly green garden towards a swimming pool. Miss Bateman sat beside it, sheltered from the sun by a blue and white striped umbrella. On a table in front of her was a large pitcher of iced fruit juice and several tumblers, as well as a tape recorder and notebook.

'You see, I've already started work,' the old woman greeted Abby. 'If anyone tells you creativity dies with age, you'll be able to refute the suggestion!'

'But you're a phenomenon,' her nephew teased before Abby could reply.

'If having one's health and strength and loving one's work is phenomenal, then you're right. But too many people use their years as an excuse to sit back and do nothing. Don't ever fall into that trap, Giles. Doing work that you enjoy keeps you young in heart.'

'But how many of us enjoy our work?' he questioned.

'You do—so don't pretend otherwise. Sometimes I think you've substituted work for everything else.'

'I made my decision years ago,' he said, and turned away.

His aunt glanced quickly at Abby, smiled and then concentrated on her nephew again. 'You can't seriously mean to live as a bachelor for the rest of your life?'

'I most seriously do.'

'What about Farrow Engineering and the money you'll get from me?'

'There are many deserving charities.' His voice was cold. 'Now, if you've finished commenting on my life, I've work to do.'

'Hoity-toity!' his aunt reproved. 'Are you lunching in?'

'No. I'll see you at dinner.'

'But you are going to escort us to Mr Chandris's party?'

'Do you think you're well enough to go?' he queried.

'Stop trying to make an invalid of me! I haven't seen the Chandrises since they were in London and I'm looking forward to meeting them again.'

'I can always ask them to dine here with us one evening.'

'For goodness' sake,' his aunt snorted, 'I want to go *out*!'

With a shrug he left them and Abby settled on a chair. Since she was accepting Giles Farrow's hospitality—grudging though it was—she supposed that from this moment on her employment had begun. But she was not sure what it entailed. Miss Bateman had said secretarial work, and she glanced at the tape recorder.

'If there's a typewriter here, I can start transcribing the cassette.'

'During your holiday? My dear child, I'm not a slavedriver!' A smile multiplied the wrinkles on Miss Bateman's face. 'You may have left the Gallway and King tour, but your private one has only begun.'

'My private tour?' Abby was puzzled. 'What do you mean?'

'Never you mind. Treat it as a mystery.' The brown eyes gleamed. 'After all, I'm a mystery writer!'

Not sure if she was being teased, Abby looked uncertain. 'I'd feel much happier if I could do *some* work for you while we're here. If I don't, I'll feel guilty for not staying at a hotel.'

'Twaddle!' Miss Bateman went on eyeing her. 'Very well,' she said at last. 'You can appease your conscience if it pricks you so badly. But if you intend becoming my employee as of now, you'll have to obey me implicitly.'

Abby knew there was a hidden meaning behind this

statement, but was aware that Miss Bateman had no intention of revealing what it was.

'You're a bossy old woman,' she grinned. 'And I'll only obey you if I agree with the command!'

Miss Bateman sighed. 'I can see I've engaged myself a little dragon! But never mind, you're such a charming one. I only wish you could charm Giles.'

Abby coloured and quickly changed the subject. 'What happened to your previous secretary?' she asked.

'She ran off with some money of mine. She was desperately hard up for money—not for herself but for some scallywag she was engaged to. I had hoped that if she stayed with me long enough she would see him for the scoundrel he was, but unfortunately she didn't.'

'What happened to her? I hope you got your money back.'

'I didn't even try. Giles wanted me to prosecute, but I wouldn't. The money she took was unimportant to me and obviously meant a great deal to her.'

'How can you be so forgiving?' asked Abby.

'Why shouldn't I be? She'll be more hurt by her actions than I will be.'

Abby digested this comment. 'I'm surprised you engaged me without taking up any references,' she said.

'My dear, you're as transparent as glass!'

'How dull you make me sound!'

The dark eyes twinkled. 'I didn't say plain glass.'

Abby laughed and jumped to her feet. She went over to the pool. Her body cast a shadow on the water and as a breeze rippled the surface, her shadow became distorted.

'I wish I were tall and blonde,' she said, swinging

her arms wide, 'or raven-haired and dramatic instead of an ordinary mouse.'

'Not an *ordinary* mouse,' Miss Bateman chided. 'One with honey-gold hair and serene brown eyes. You must stop thinking of yourself in a derogatory way. I've told you that before.'

Abby wiped her brow free of perspiration. 'It's hot out here. I would like to change into something cooler.'

'Go round the garden to the kitchen. You'll find Indira there. She's the cook and runs the entire house.'

Abby nodded and made her way round the marble-clad walls till the smell of curry told her she was approaching the kitchen. The back door was wide open and a young girl in a saffron-coloured sari was busy pounding spices with a pestle and mortar. As she saw Abby she gave a shy smile and called out in a sibilant tongue which brought forth an amazingly fat woman from behind a cupboard door.

'Yes, missis,' she asked, 'you want tea?'

'No, thanks,' Abby smiled. 'I'm looking for my bedroom. I'm Miss Bateman's secretary and she told me to come here and ask for Indira.'

'I am Indira.' The fat woman beckoned Abby inside and led her through the large but old-fashioned kitchen back into the main hall, where a stentorian shout brought a manservant running.

'Why you not show missis to her room?' the cook scolded.

Lowering his head as if chastened, he led Abby up the winding marble staircase to a vast bedroom overlooking the garden. The furniture was as large as the proportions of the room required, the bed big enough to house a family, and the wardrobe so enormous that every single item she owned—apparel and furniture—

would have disappeared in its interior. Gold brocade curtains hung stiffly at the windows and thick Indian rugs were underfoot. A door on the left disclosed a bathroom, with king-size tub of pink marble and gold-plated taps that matched the thick yellow towels.

Quickly Abby unpacked, showered, slipped on a fresh dress and returned to the garden again, where Miss Bateman was scribbling in a notebook.

'How does *Murder by an Air Bubble* appeal to you?'

'Murder never appeals to me,' Abby said without thinking, then looked so disgusted that her employer laughed.

'I take it you aren't a fan of mine?'

'Actually I am. But I read your books because I enjoy your characterisation more than the murders you make your characters commit.'

'That's exactly what Giles says.' The notebook closed with a snap. 'I hope you've something pretty to wear tonight, Abby. The Chandrises always give delightful parties and I'm sure you'll enjoy yourself.'

'You weren't thinking of taking me?' Abby asked in alarm.

'But of course. You are my companion as well as my secretary, and I expect you to go everywhere with me.' Head on one side, she surveyed Abby. 'You'd look nice in a sari. Would you be willing to wear one?'

'How would the Indians feel about it?' asked Abby.

'They would be flattered.'

'Then my answer is yes.'

'I have several,' Miss Bateman said. 'They're just simple lengths of material, five or six metres long. But you need to wear a special right-fitting blouse and a long straight skirt underneath it. I'll have Lala measure you and make them.'

'Lala?' queried Abby.

'The upstairs maid. She's an excellent seamstress. Come on, child.'

Intrigued at the prospect of what lay ahead, Abby followed Miss Bateman to her bedroom, where a ring on the bell brought a slender Indian girl gliding in to see them. She was a few years older than Abby, with such fine features she could have posed for any one of the delicate Indian miniatures that lined the walls of the room. Miss Bateman told her what was wanted and she disappeared, returning again with a tape measure. With gentle, bird-like movements she took Abby's measurements, looked at her carefully and then left.

'You will have your blouse and skirt by five o'clock this evening,' Miss Bateman smiled. 'Now comes the nice part—choosing which sari length you would like.'

She pointed to a tall chest of drawers. It was made of dark wood and intricately inlaid with ivory : a valuable museum piece. Carefully Abby opened the top drawer, gasping with delight as she saw the jewel-like materials that lay within. There were gossamer silks, heavier brocades, and gauzy nets encrusted with pearls and sequins. The colours ranged through the rainbow and Abby shook her head in bewilderment.

'I'm spoilt for choice,' she murmured.

'Then let me decide.' Miss Bateman marched over, regarded the drawer and then pulled out a length of deep rose silk bordered with gold. She held it up against Abby and nodded. 'The colour is excellent for your skin; it gives it a glow.'

Holding the material against her, Abby went over to the mirror dressing-table. She lacked the imagination to know how it would look like when draped into a sari and knew she would have to accept Miss Bateman's judgment.

Later that evening she conceded that the choice of colour had been an inspired one. It did indeed make her skin glow and drew attention to its pearly quality. Even her hair seemed to take on an added lustre, and unexpected glints of gold appeared in the silk tresses. Intrigued, she watched as Lala skilfully manoeuvred the sari length into pleats, pinning them with tiny gold safety pins and then draping the whole length round Abby's waist, inserting it into the tight waistband of the long skirt she had just made. A few more skilful twists and then five metres of silk were transformed into a flowing graceful garment that gave her small form an elegance she had never noticed before.

'Many European women love to wear saris,' said Lala in her lilting voice. 'But many do not look good in it. One must be small-boned, like you.'

Abby accepted the remark as a fact and not as a compliment.

'I must try to glide when I move,' she smiled. 'Swinging arms and a firm gait don't go with a sari!'

Lala looked at her questioningly and Abby marched round the room to show her what she meant, which made the Indian girl lean back on her heels and rock with mirth. Abby slowed her pace and moved in small, even steps.

'Very good,' said Lala. 'You are a perfect Indian lady.'

Abby went back to the mirror and surveyed herself. 'There's still something missing,' she said, head on one side, 'but I don't know what it is.'

Without replying, Lala put up her hand to her own neck and ears and quickly unclipped the gold necklace and long dangling ear-rings which she handed to Abby.

'Please borrow them,' she said. 'I think you will find that this is what is missing.'

Abby did as the girl suggested and saw at once that Lala was right. 'It's kind of you to lend me them,' she smiled. 'Thank you.'

'Tomorrow I will tell you where to go to buy the same,' said Lala. 'They are not expensive.'

'But they're too ornate to wear with Western dress, and I can't see myself wearing a sari again.'

'You can buy a plainer set. You look so lovely in them.'

Abby fingered the delicate chandelier ear-rings. There was something provocative about them that gave her a devil-may-care feeling. Jewellery and clothes had an effect on one's behaviour and, thinking of her serviceable cottons, she knew an urge to consign them to the garbage can.

'Doesn't wearing this kind of jewellery indicate that you're married?' she asked, pointing to the necklace round her throat.

'Not always. A beauty mark is a much surer sign.' Lala lowered her head to show a rouge mark where her hair was parted in the centre.

'I didn't know you were married,' Abby said in surprise.

'For eleven years.'

'That's impossible! You aren't older than I am.'

'I am twenty-four. I was betrothed to my husband when I was three and I married him when I was thirteen.'

Abby looked at Lala with sadness. What sort of life did a woman have when she was betrothed to a man she did not know and then married to him when she was still a child? Yet as a stranger in this country, it was politic to hold her counsel.

'Do you have any children, Lala?' she asked.

'Two boys. My mother-in-law looks after them during the day.' The brown eyes held amusement. 'You are not yet betrothed?'

Abby grinned. 'I don't even have a boy-friend.'

'Does it worry you?'

'Not so far. I've just got myself a wonderful job with Miss Bateman.' Only Giles Farrow could be a thorn in her flesh, but she could not say this to Lala. Nor should she even think it. She must put the man out of her mind.

'Perhaps you will find love soon,' said Lala. 'In this sari you will attract many male eyes.'

Abby's own eyes glinted with humour. 'Especially if I trip on my skirt! I'll go down and give myself some practice.'

Bowing gracefully, Lala collected her bag of pins and glided out, a movement which Abby tried to emulate for the next half hour.

By the time she carefully descended the stairs she was more or less successful, and she made her way somewhat diffidently into the salon. The room was deserted and she breathed a sigh of relief at the reprieve. It wasn't what Miss Bateman would say about her appearance that worried her but what Giles Farrow's reaction would be. Nervously she went to the window and looked out into the dusk-filled garden, where soft lights glowed among the shrubbery. There was a slight sound and she turned to see the man who, only a moment ago, had been occupying her thoughts.

He wore black trousers and a cream-coloured dinner jacket. As he came closer she saw it was silk, several shades darker than the fine cream shirt through which his bronze skin gleamed faintly. There was an elusive hint of shaving lotion as he moved and she was more strongly aware of him than at any other time since they had met : possibly because he was scrutinising her with frank amusement.

'So the moth has shed her chrysalis and turned into a butterfly!'

She half smiled. 'Actually I feel like Cinderella.'

'But unlike Cinderella, you won't have to change back into rags at midnight. This finery remains with you, no doubt.' He pointed to the shimmering pink silk that caressed her body and subtly revealed her curves. 'A present from my aunt?'

Her cheeks matched the colour of her sari. 'How clever of you to guess.'

'Not cleverness, Miss West. It's happened too many times before. My aunt picks up strays the way a dog picks up fleas. She lavishes everything she possibly can on them, then sits back while they bite her hand.'

All Abby's good intentions not to lose her temper dissolved in the face of this unwarranted attack.

'Since you only insult me when you talk to me, Mr Farrow, I would be obliged if you kept your conversation with me to the minimum.'

'Do you find the truth objectionable?' he drawled.

'Not the truth,' she snapped. 'But I object to being judged by other people's shortcomings.'

The tightening of his jaw told her she had annoyed him, yet his body remained relaxed as he leaned against the back of a chair, one hand in the pocket of his jacket. 'I don't believe in buying affection or loyalty.'

'Nor do I,' she said. 'Anyway, genuine affection and loyalty can't be bought, it comes naturally.'

'The way yours does for my aunt?'

'I haven't known your aunt long enough to feel either,' Abby said with spirit. 'So don't use your cleverness to try to trap me. I know you think I had an ulterior purpose in looking after her in Agra, but I would have done the same for anyone who needed help —even you.'

His eyebrows rose. 'Little Miss Do-Gooder! I'll bear it in mind when I feel in need of succour.'

She moved as though to walk past him, but he had already turned away to greet his aunt as she came through the door. In long black silk, she looked far more elegant than at any time since Abby had seen her, though she mischievously lifted the skirts of her dress to disclose that she was wearing her usual old black shoes.

'Comfort before fashion,' she explained and, dropping her skirt, surveyed the girl in front of her. 'You look beautiful, my dear.' She glanced at her nephew. 'Don't you think so, Giles?'

'I wouldn't describe Miss West as beautiful.'

'How ungallant of you! How would you describe her, then?'

Scarlet-faced, Abby waited for him to reply. The edges of his mouth lifted sardonically and he gave her the full benefit of his strange amber eyes, though when he spoke, the words were addressed to his aunt.

'I would describe her as a small pink candle,' he said. 'The kind that you place on Buddhist shrines.'

'What do you think of that for a compliment?' Miss Bateman asked Abby.

'I think Mr Farrow is hoping that, like a candle, I'll melt away!'

'Is that true, Giles?' his aunt asked mischievously.

'I haven't given Miss West any thought.'

Giles Farrow's voice was so indifferent that Abby longed to do him a physical violence. Never had a man aroused such feeling of rage in her as this one did.

'We'd better leave,' he went on calmly, and led the way to the waiting car.

CHAPTER EIGHT

THE Chandrises lived in one of Bombay's newest apartment blocks, built on the winding shore that bordered the Indian Ocean. Gliding down the steep road from Malibar Hill, Giles Farrow's limousine skirted the Hanging Gardens and turned left to give the occupants a sweeping view of the city set out below them.

It was only as it turned again that Abby saw the high wall to one side of the road, beyond which lay the small parkland in which was situated the cylindrical Towers of Silence. It was here that the Parsee dead were left to be devoured by waiting vultures, Giles Farrow casually told her, adding that the birds plucked a body clean within an hour.

Abby could not repress a shiver which Miss Bateman saw at once. 'I know it seems a barbarous custom to us,' she said quietly, 'but the Parsees are Zoroastrian and that means they respect all elements of nature, including fire and earth. That's why they cannot pollute the earth with their corpses the way Christians do, nor burn them on funeral pyres like the Hindus.'

'But surely they needn't have put their—their cemetery and vultures in the middle of the city?' Abby protested.

'Money speaks loudly.' Giles came back into the conversation. 'The Parsees built Bombay trade and industry. There are only a hundred and fifteen thousand of them in India, which in a country of five hundred million is absolutely negligible, yet they're the leading businessmen and possess the greatest wealth.'

'Then they can afford to re-site their death house somewhere else.'

'I'm sure you're right, Miss West. But tradition dies hard, and the Towers of Silence are likely to remain where they are for a long time to come.'

Pointedly Abby said nothing and focused her attention on the passing scene. They were bowling along the seashore, where block after block of apartments reared into the sky, all of them modern and concrete and totally unlike the embellished Victorian architecture that abounded in the inner regions of the city. People were already taking their evening promenade: coconut hawkers from Kerala in ankle-length white robes; children with begging bowls and the distended bellies of hunger; crowds of young men returning home from a day's work.

Marine Drive was long and seemingly never-ending, and the bustling throngs only started to diminish as they came towards its end. Here stood the newest built apartment house, looming high into the darkening Bombay sky. The limousine stopped and they emerged from it, breathed in the humid sea air and then entered through sliding glass doors into a world where poverty was not known.

'The Chandrises built this block,' Miss Bateman explained, 'and they live on the two top floors.'

'They must have a large family,' Abby exclaimed.

'All their children are married and no longer live with them!'

'I thought some children always lived with their parents?'

'Not in the wealthy families, particularly if they're Westernised. The close-knit unity of family that one finds in the villages doesn't indicate a greater love for each other, but merely force of circumstance. When one is poor, it's cheaper to live together. But the Chandrises only have two sons; both of whom are attached to the U.N. in New York.'

Wondering how a middle-aged couple could occupy two entire floors of a building such as this, Abby entered the lift which swiftly took them to the top floor.

'This is their summer entrance,' Miss Bateman explained as they stepped out on to a vast terrace, complete with swimming pool and an elaborately laid out garden. 'During the monsoons one gets out on the floor below, which is covered.'

'A winter and summer entrance,' Abby grinned. 'I bet they have a his and hers bathroom too!'

'And a yours and theirs as well!' came the amused rejoinder as Miss Bateman and her nephew led the way towards a cluster of people who parted to allow them to meet the couple who stood in their midst.

Mr Chandris was a rotund, white-haired man with a sallow complexion and deep-set eyes, and his wife a graceful woman with the same white hair but lighter skin. She wore a white sari of the utmost simplicity, which acted as a foil for the glittering array of diamonds around her throat and dangling from the lobes of her ears. They both spoke perfect English, though with the lilting Welsh accent which so many Indians seemed to have. Then Abby found herself being escorted to the buffet by a black-haired young man with liquid brown eyes who regarded her admiringly as he helped her to a drink.

He was an accountant named Jay, and worked in one of Mr Chandris's many firms. He was also a cousin of

the family and knew most of the guests already present.
He pointed out several Indian notabilities to her, including two film stars who were, to Abby's European
eyes, overweight and surprisingly ugly.

There were some hundred people present, but the
terrace and living-rooms were so enormous that neither
was overcrowded. From time to time, servants in long
brocade jackets with sashes at their waists plied them
with small bowls of aromatic curry as well as trays of
Western-style canapés. There was also a continuous
supply of champagne for those who had no religious
scruples, and varied fruit juice for those who had.

Abby glanced at her young escort who was sipping
fruit juice. 'Have you never drunk wine?' she asked.

'I used to do so when I was in England. I got my
degree at London University, but now I live with my
uncle, and he is a very devout Parsee.'

'Aren't you?'

'I am becoming more so.' He smiled and she smiled
back, thinking how good-looking he was in his high-
collared white tunic with matching tight-fitting
trousers. His head was uncovered, but she noticed that
many of the men present wore small white caps, and
seeing her eyes rest on them he explained that this
indicated that the wearer was a member or follower of
the Ruling Congress Party. All the Indian women were
in saris, the majority of them lavishly embroidered,
and there was a mass of jewellery, as there always was
among Indian women. Abby, who had felt remarkably
different in her own sari, now regretted she was not
wearing Western dress, though as she turned to say so
to her escort he forestalled her by saying how charming
she looked.

'It is such a compliment to us when a Western

woman wears a sari. And you do it so well.'

'I felt very ungainly for the first few minutes,' she confessed.

'I can't believe that. You glided across the terrace like a swan.'

Had the remark come from an Italian or a Frenchman, he would have continued with the compliment, but Indians, Abby knew from what she had seen and read, were far more reserved in their attitude towards women, and treated them with the respect that their European counterparts had long since forgotten. In India, women were considered the centre of the home and family life, and since family life was all-important here, it was natural for them to be revered. It was this reverence that had contributed to the Indian male's acceptance of marriage without love, for he was willing to commit himself for life to a woman as long as he knew she had been chosen by his parents as being a suitable partner for him.

'If you are happy in your home, then you will love the woman who makes that home with you,' one of the young guides had explained to Abby on her second day in Delhi. He had been the best guide of them all. Studying law at Delhi University, he was only a guide during the holidays, and had told them that he was perfectly content to marry a girl of his parents' choice, whom he himself would meet for the first time upon their wedding day.

Abby wondered whether the man beside her would do the same, but thought it overly curious—on such a short acquaintance—to ask him.

'Would you care for another drink?' Jay enquired.

'Not for the moment, thanks.'

He turned to get himself another fruit juice and, as

his shoulder moved, she had a clear view of the panelled gold doors of the lift. They slid back and a group of Indians emerged. The two Europeans in their midst caught her eye; not so much the man—who was middle-aged and balding—but the woman with him, who was one of the most beautiful creatures Abby had seen. She was tall and slim as a wand, with soft dark hair swinging in a thick satin cloud to touch the edge of her jawline, where the ends swung forward provocatively on to each cheek. Her features had the classical purity Abby always associated with Russian ballerinas and she walked with the same grace too, her body seen to advantage in a simple amber gold dress.

The colour was exactly the same as Giles Farrow's eyes, and because of it Abby glanced across to where he was standing talking to the Chandrises. As she watched him the European couple came into his line of vision, and he lost colour so sharply that it was visible even from a distance. Even his stance changed, growing so rigid that his flesh might have been stone.

Swiftly Abby turned her attention to the couple who had just come in. The girl had stopped walking, but only momentarily, for as Abby watched, she started to move in the direction of her host and hostess, and greeted them with a smile before turning to Giles Farrow. He was more in control of himself now, though Abby saw that his hands were clenched by his side.

Without having to be told, she knew this was his ex-fiancée; the girl who had turned him down because she had been unable to face the prospect of life in small Indian towns. She glanced around at Jay, who had also noticed the newcomers.

'Who are the Western couple?' she asked.

'Tony Laughton and his wife. He's an oil tycoon. He

and my uncle have many business dealings together. His wife is extremely beautiful, is she not?'

'Extremely,' Abby said slowly. 'What is her first name?'

'Victoria. It is appropriate, because she is English!'

'Victoria,' Abby murmured, and was convinced this was the Vicky of whom Miss Bateman had spoken that morning. Again she looked across to Giles Farrow. He had regained control of himself and was smiling with exactly the right amount of ease, one hand in the pocket of his jacket, the other loosely clasped around a glass tumbler. Unwillingly she gave him full marks for his performance, appreciating the effort it cost him to appear natural. Or had he known his ex-fiancée was coming here tonight? Remembering the stricken look on his face as the girl had entered the room, Abby doubted it. No, her appearance had been a shock to him, but one which he was now managing to hide.

As Abby continued to look at the group, Miss Bateman joined it. Her eyes met Abby's and she lifted her hand and beckoned her. Smiling an apology to the young Indian at her side, Abby obeyed the command.

'I would like you to meet the Laughtons,' Miss Bateman said as Abby reached her. 'Vicky is a friend of the family.'

'Nearly a member of the family,' the dark girl corrected, her mouth curving in a smile that still left her eyes humourless.

It was apparent from the hard look in them that she was annoyed at being described in this way, and though Miss Bateman looked unaware of it, the slight tensing of her fingers, which were still resting on Abby's arm, gave her away.

'Well,' she said cheerily, 'as a near member of the

family, I'd like you to meet the dear girl who came to my rescue when I was taken ill in Agra.'

The hardness in Vicky Laughton's eyes remained as they rested on Abby. 'So you were the Good Samaritan?' she drawled. 'And now I hear you're working for Aunt Matty. How clever of you!'

Abby wasn't sure what to say in reply. She sensed an undercurrent of antagonism in the statement, and wondered what she had done to arouse it. The answer was given immediately, for Vicky Laughton turned her head and looked directly at Giles.

'You'd better be on your guard, Giles. I think Aunt Matty is matchmaking!'

'My guard is permanently up,' he said calmly.

'Do you mean I was the only one who ever got through your defence?'

Astonished by the girl's cruelty, Abby turned away. But she could still hear Giles' reply, which was measured and devoid of expression.

'I didn't have any guard up at the time I met you. I erected it afterwards.'

'Now you've made me feel guilty.' This time the girl did lower her voice, but Abby could still hear what she said. 'Have you forgiven me?' she went on softly.

'I forgave you immediately. One can't blame a child for doing wrong—if the child has never been taught what is right.'

Vicky Laughton's exclamation was difficult to define. It was part anger, part exasperation, and with a deliberate movement she turned away. Only then did Giles Farrow move a step in Abby's direction.

'I hope you're enjoying the party, Miss West?'

'Very much. It's the first time I've been in an Indian home.'

Her answer seemed to amuse him, for one side of his

HOTEL D

New From

Harlequin

the leading publisher of Romantic Fiction

What secrets lie within the Hotel De La Marine?

For weeks the small French fishing village of Port Royal had been aflame with rumors about the mysterious stranger. Why had he come? What was he after? Challenged by his haughty, yet haunted demeanor, Marie was determined to break through his mask of indifference. But he was as charming as he was cunning, uncanny in perception and driven by vengeance. From the moment she learned his secret, Marie lived with the fear of discovery, and the thrill of danger.

Uncover those secrets with Marie in the gripping pages of *High Wind in Brittany* by *Caroline Gayet*—one of the many best-selling authors of romantic suspense presented by Mystique Books.

MYSTIQUES

Now every month you can be spellbound by 4 exciting Mystique novels like these. You'll be swept away to casinos in Monte Carlo, ski chalets in the Alps, or mysterious ruins in Mexico. You'll experience the excitement of intrigue and the warmth of romance. Mystique novels are all written by internationally acclaimed, best-selling authors of romantic suspense.

Subscribe now! As a member of the Mystiques Subscription plan, you'll receive 4 books each month. Cancel anytime. And still keep your 4 FREE BOOKS!

mouth tilted. 'This hardly typifies an Indian home. It could be the home of any rich cosmopolitan.'

Abby looked over his shoulder at the huge living room, with its gay rugs and multi-coloured brass and glass lamps. 'Surely not?' she protested.

'Kashmiri carpets and mosaic gew-gaws don't make an Indian home,' he replied. 'My own home is more typically Indian than this, and that's because the Maharajah, who owns it, was never influenced by Europe.'

'Except for the plumbing,' she smiled. 'That's almost American in its proficiency!'

'Do you consider plumbing an important part of life?'

'Don't you?'

'Important but not essential. I've spent too much time in small Indian villages where plumbing didn't exist to believe one can't live without it.'

'I'm sure one can live,' she agreed. 'But it's a question of the quality of living. There are certain comforts that I consider essential.'

'I'm sure,' he said sourly. 'You're no different from any other woman.'

Immediately she knew he was thinking of Vicky Laughton. But since she was not supposed to know about his engagement, nor why it had been broken, she looked at him with pretended innocence. 'I'm not saying I wouldn't be able to rough it; under certain circumstances I would.'

'What circumstances?' he asked.

To answer him truthfully and say she would do it if it meant being with someone she loved would make it sound as if she knew about his past; worse, it would make her sound as if she wanted to put herself in a good light with him; and since both these ideas were repugnant to her, she said nothing.

'You're very easy to read, Miss West,' Giles said into the silence. 'In your romantic mind you can see yourself sharing all sorts of dire hardships with the man of your choice. But when it comes to the reality of life, you'd find civilisation too attractive to give up.'

'I certainly wouldn't want to give it up permanently. But nor would you. I mean, you're living pretty well now, so why blame others for wanting the same?'

'Because *I* have my priorities right. There are other things which have far more meaning for me than plumbing.'

'And for other people too, Mr Farrow. Since time immemorial, men have gone out into the wilds to bring religion, education, technical benefits, to people less fortunate than themselves. What you're doing isn't so extraordinary.'

She hadn't meant to say so much, but as always when she was emotionally aroused, her tongue ran away with her. There was no doubt Giles Farrow thought so too, for he looked at her with his all too familiar irritation.

'I dislike people who jump on a soapbox at the first opportunity,' he said.

'You mean you dislike anyone who feels strongly enough about something to make a stand!'

'If you want to put it that way, yes!'

'Don't you yourself take a stand on things you feel deeply about?'

He nodded. 'But I don't condemn others if they don't want to do the same. For my part, I don't give a damn what other people do.'

'Then I'm not surprised that no one—except your aunt—gives a damn what you do!'

Anger blazed from his eyes, making them glow like

those of a tiger in the night. Abby waited for his temper to explode, but she had reckoned without his self-control.

'I have no need of everyone's good opinion of me, Miss West. As long as I am liked by the few people I respect, I am satisfied. But *your* good opinion of me doesn't matter.'

Her eyes stung sharply with tears, and appalled lest he see them, she walked over to the edge of the terrace. Blindly she stared out at the ocean, too high above it to hear the sound of the surf on the sand.

'Miss West?' Giles Farrow came to stand by her side and, as she backed away from him, he blocked her escape. 'Please forgive me for what I just said. It was unforgivable of me to speak to you like that.'

'You have been rude to me from the moment we met,' she said in a voice that trembled.

'But not as rude as I was now,' he said raggedly. 'My only excuse is that ... there are things on my mind and I'm on edge. Please accept my apology.'

'Very well.'

Only then did she glance at him, and had to tilt her head a long way to do so. He was not as pale as he had been when he had first glimpsed Vicky Laughton, but he had not yet regained his normal colour and his paleness made him look younger and more vulnerable.

'It's a pity I have to stay in your home,' she added. 'I'll try to keep out of your way as much as I can.'

'That isn't necessary.'

'I *want* to.'

He opened his mouth as though to say more, then clamped it shut. 'As you wish,' he murmured, and strode away.

Abby remained where she was, wishing that Giles

Farrow did not have the ability to make her dislike him and feel sorry for him at one and the same time. Like a summer storm their quarrel had arisen without any warning, and like a summer storm it had disappeared as quickly as it had come. Yet it had left behind a residue of pain that made her deeply afraid, for she did not want to acknowledge that a man like Giles Farrow had the ability to hurt her. What he made of his life and what he thought of other people was not her concern, nor did it matter to her whether he held her in esteem or contempt. Once she left Bombay she would have no reason to see him. When he returned to England and visited his aunt, she would make sure she was not present, if his visits became too frequent, she would resign her job.

She turned and saw Giles Farrow standing by the terrace window, his body outlined by the light behind him. He was considerably taller than any of the Indian men present and for this reason alone would have stood out among them. Yet it was not his height alone that set him apart; it was his air of command; the look of a man who was in control of himself as well as others; a man who thought with his head and never with his heart.

Refusing to think of him any longer, she went to rejoin Miss Bateman.

'Would you be very disappointed if we left the party now?' the woman asked as Abby reached her side.

'Not at all. I'm ready when you are.'

'Then we'll go down and ask the porter to find us a taxi.'

'Won't Mr Farrow wonder what's happened to you?'

'I'll see that a message is sent to him when it's too late for him to come after us.'

'You've planned everything,' Abby smiled.

'I always do,' came the retort, and the thin arm slipped itself through Abby's and edged her to the door.

It was not until they were in a ramshackle taxi speeding back to Malibar Hill that the old lady spoke of Vicky Laughton.

'I suppose you guessed she was once engaged to my nephew?'

'Yes, I did. Did he know she'd be there tonight?'

'No. I don't think he even knew she was in India. You should have seen his face when she came out on the terrace.'

'I did see it,' Abby confessed. 'He seemed rather surprised.'

'Shattered is the word. But I'm glad it's happened. I told him only the other day that he should stop running away from the past and admit that he'd made an ass of himself even to have loved Vicky in the first place.'

'Seeing her could have the opposite effect and make him realise he *still* loves her,' Abby warned.

'If he does, he'll be able to do something about it. Vicky is bored with her husband and is ready to leave him.'

'Did she say so?' Abby asked, wondering when her employer could have had such an intimate conversation with the girl.

'Of course not. But I know her so well that I can tell what's in her mind before she even admits it to herself. Mark my words, Abby, she came to India to show Giles she's ready to return to him.'

'He may accept the offer,' Abby pointed out.

'He's a fool if he does. She was never good enough for him, but he loved her too much to see it. I'm hoping that all these years away from her have given him better vision.'

Abby did not answer and they drove some way in

silence before Miss Bateman spoke again.

'You think I shouldn't interfere in my nephew's life, don't you?'

'Yes,' Abby admitted. 'Loving someone doesn't give you the right to tell them what to do.'

'I wouldn't dream of telling Giles—that would be the best way of getting him to do the opposite. All I can do is to put a lovely girl in front of him and hope he'll remember he's a man.'

Abby caught her breath and Miss Bateman heard it and nodded.

'Yes, my dear. You would make Giles an ideal wife.'

'But you can't ... it's—it's awful ... I would never have agreed to work for you if I'd known such an idea was in your mind!'

'Unfortunately it doesn't seem to be in my nephew's.'

'I'm not so sure. I think he *has* guessed. That's probably why he dislikes me. Have you done this sort of thing before?'

'Many times.' The reply was blunt. 'But I've always failed.'

'You'll fail again,' Abby said with asperity. 'I really don't think I can stay with you.'

'Of course you can.' Miss Bateman clasped her wrist. 'Forgive me for being such an interfering old woman, but I love Giles and I am also becoming very fond of *you*. I shouldn't have told you what was in my mind, but seeing Vicky tonight made me lose my temper. Please forget what I said. Don't make any hasty decisions because of a foolish old woman's day-dreams.'

'But I can't continue to work for you. Every time I see Mr Farrow I shall be embarrassed.'

'Twaddle! You call yourself a modern young woman, don't you? If you're not attracted to him, you've no cause to be embarrassed.'

'That's true.' Abby almost snapped the words. 'I find your nephew quite intolerable, and I assure you he feels the same about me.'

'Then neither of you need worry about my matchmaking,' Miss Bateman said practically.

Abby could not help chuckling at how the old lady had turned the tables on her.

'You're incorrigible,' she said aloud, 'and I'll only stay with you if you promise not to do anything that will embarrass me. You must treat me as an employee and not as—as someone you'd like to have as a niece.'

'If that's what you want,' came the prompt reply, 'then that's what you'll have.'

Lying in bed an hour later, Abby found it hard to forget her conversation with Miss Bateman. Knowing the woman had seen her as a potential wife for her nephew made it all too easy for Abby to see herself in the same way, and it was disquieting to discover how agreable the picture was. If only Giles Farrow's character matched his extreme good looks! Perhaps if he had never met Vicky Laughton ... Yet to think he might have been different was pure conjecture, for she had never seen any side to him other than an irritable one.

Tyres scraped on the drive below her window and headlights gleamed momentarily on the wall opposite her bed. Giles had come home. She heard the car door slam and then the front door follow it. After that there was silence, for the walls were thick. But the knowledge that he was so close re-awakened the embarrassment she had felt earlier. Could she continue to stay here? Would she be able to see him without remembering his accusation that she was here for the pickings she could get from his aunt? And was he afraid she might be hoping to pluck *him*? Surprisingly she giggled.

If that was what he thought, she was going to take great pleasure to show him he was wrong. The last thing she wanted for herself was a man who had allowed himself to be permanently soured by another woman.

On this determined thought she fell asleep.

CHAPTER NINE

FOR the next fortnight Abby ostentatiously avoided Giles Farrow. On the infrequent occasions when he dined at home with his aunt, she would sit at the table like a deaf mute and glide away from it immediately the meal was over. She developed a sixth sense that told her when he was in the house or about to return to it, and almost before his car stopped in the drive, she was halfway up the stairs to her room, where she would remain until Miss Bateman asked to see her or the gong summoned her to a meal.

To begin with, Giles Farrow tried to engage her in conversation, as if still trying to atone for his rudeness at the party, but soon realised what her attitude was and decided to ignore her. Only on the evenings when he was not at home did Abby feel sufficiently at ease to wander around the downstairs rooms and admire the beautiful paintings, furniture and *objets d'art*, repeatedly returning to study the miniatures that lined the wall of what had obviously been the Maharajah's private sitting-room.

It was not much used these days, for Miss Bateman preferred to sit under the shade of the trees in the garden during the day and in the salon at night, with its screened doors opening on to the arched patio. But Abby loved the little sitting-room with its puffy cushions, rich textured carpet and heavily embossed walls, one of which was completely covered with the miniatures. She longed to reproduce one of them and the urge to do so sent her searching on the main shopping street for watercolour paper and paints. That night, to her great pleasure, Giles Farrow was again dining out, and after she and Miss Bateman had finished their meal she went to the little sitting-room, draped a cloth over one of the small, intricately carved tables, to protect it, and set her paper and paints on it.

She had already chosen the miniature she wanted to copy, and she carefully took it down from the wall and placed it on another table beside her. Ever since she could remember she had possessed the ability to copy fluently, and occasionally wondered whether she might not have achieved success and job satisfaction if she had become a picture restorer.

She lowered her head and began to draw, pink tongue between small white teeth, her whole face and body absorbed in her task. Swiftly the picture began to take shape, the small figures forming themselves in front of her as if they were rolling out of her pencil. In less than an hour the outline was done, and she picked up one of her brushes and loaded it with paint. As she put the first touch of colour on to the smooth surface of the paper, she let out a sigh of pure sensual pleasure and then held her brush motionless in order to savour this moment. It was only then, as she raised her head from the table, that she saw Giles Farrow.

Her heart started to pound as if she were a thief who had been caught in the act of stealing, and she set her brush down carefully on the box of paints and went to rise.

'Don't let my presence send you away,' he said quietly.

'I was going to stop anyway.'

'May I see what you're doing?'

Short of being openly rude, which she had resolved not to be, it was impossible to refuse. 'Do you mind if I don't lift the paper, it's still wet?'

He nodded and came over to the table, looking first at the miniature and then at her copy of it. 'I hadn't realised you were an artist.'

'I'm not. I'm a copyist.'

'And an excellent one.' He bent closer, his face intent. 'You've got every single detail. How long have you been doing it?'

'I started after dinner.'

'It has the accuracy of a photograph. If you paint it as well as you've drawn it, it will be a perfect reproduction.'

She remained unresponsive and he straightened and moved across to the window that overlooked the secluded part of the garden.

'Have you sold any of your reproductions?' he asked.

'I generally give them away.'

He swung round to look at her, a gleam in his eye. 'Are you doing this as a present for my aunt?'

'No. I don't think Miss Bateman would appreciate it; not when she can afford the real thing.' Anger made her continue, even though she knew that when it abated she would regret what she was saying.

'The last copy I made of a picture was Gainsborough's *Blue Boy*. It was a favourite of an old woman whose shopping I do. She used to go to the Gallery once a month to look at it until she became too frail to travel. She bought a print reproduction, but it wasn't the same thing for her, so I made her a copy in oils. It was a totally premeditated action on my part, because I know that when she dies she'll endow me with all her worldly goods. I haven't yet told her that an old age pensioner can't bequeath her pension to anyone, because she'd be upset to hear it, since she hasn't anything else to leave me.'

Her voice shaking, Abby collapsed into silence, already bitterly regretting her lost temper. There was no reason for her to explain herself to Giles Farrow. Why should she care how badly he thought of her?

It was a question immediately echoed by what he said. 'Why did you tell me that, Miss West? I can't believe you care what I think of you.'

'I don't. But since I know you have such a low opinion, I thought I might confound you with the truth.'

'I could disbelieve you.'

This was something that had not occurred to her, and he saw it as he went on watching her face. 'Don't worry, Miss West. I do happen to believe you. No one would make up such a sentimental tale.'

Fury impelled her across the room towards him. 'Do you have to denigrate everyone?' she cried. 'You're so hard-boiled, you make a stone seem soft!'

'Too hard-boiled for you to reform me?'

'I wouldn't want to waste my time on you! You're the most contemptible man I've ever met!'

She went to swing away from him, but his hand shot out to her shoulder and swung her back to face him. 'Be careful how you talk to me. You're still a guest in my home.'

'Don't remind me! If I didn't like your aunt so much, I'd leave here tonight.'

'You mean you've given up all thought of getting anywhere with me?'

Colour ran up her neck and into her face, and the increased glitter of his golden eyes told her he had seen it and was enjoying her embarrassment.

'So you did know what my aunt was hoping for when she engaged you! I wasn't sure you did, but now you've answered me.'

Abby swallowed hard. 'I only found out the other night—after the party. If I'd guessed it in the beginning, nothing would have induced me to work for her. I may enjoy helping lame ducks, but not being sacrificed on the altar of egoism and rigidity!'

His breath hissed between his teeth and angrily he jerked her close. 'You know nothing about me. Nothing!'

'I know you're so eaten up with self-pity because a stupid girl behaved stupidly that you think every woman will act in the same way.'

'Most of them will,' he grated. 'Their main concern is to find the richest man they can.'

'That's not true!'

'Isn't it? Then why are you here? Or do you expect me to believe you really enjoy the prospect of living in the country for nine months of the year and working for a woman in her mid-seventies!'

'That's exactly what I fancy,' Abby cried. 'Living in a nunnery would be a pleasure compared with living with you!'

'Is that so?' With startling suddenness his mouth came down on hers. She struggled to free herself, but she was like a sparrow trying to free itself from an eagle, and he merely increased the pressure of his mouth and held her more tightly, forcing her lips apart by the pressure of his own.

No man had kissed her in this way before; no hands had moved over her breasts and body in such intimate gestures, and despite her burning anger she felt the insidious flame of desire kindle at his touch. Afraid he would guess how he was making her feel, she began to kick him, and he swung her against the wall and pinned her there with his body, making it impossible for her to fight him.

She was astonished that his aloof exterior hid such violent passion, and recognising the depth of the feelings she had aroused—albeit they were caused by anger and not love—she went limp in his arms, knowing that to fight him any more would make him continue to punish her.

It was only as he felt her body sag in his hold that he lifted his mouth away from hers and looked into her eyes. His pupils were dilated, so that there was only a narrow golden rim around them. She stared into them, reminded of the eclipse of the sun she had once seen, when the moon had overlain it and all that had been visible was the bright corona. Fascinated, she went on staring into his eyes and, as she did so, the pupils contracted and the golden rim widened and deepened until they became the rich warm topaz which had been the first thing she had noticed about him that morning at the airport, a lifetime ago.

Never had she suspected then that halfway across the world she would find herself held against him, her mouth bruised from the pressure of his, her body trembling from the touch of his hands. Oddly, all fear of him had gone, even though she was still pinned so tightly against him that she could feel the throbbing contractions that racked his body and slowly subsided. But she knew that the rage within him had gone. Although desire still remained, he was able to control it, and slowly he loosened his grip on her, though he continued to stare steadfastly into her eyes.

'I'm sorry, Abby. What I did was inexcusable.'

'It was as much my fault,' she said huskily. 'I goaded you into it.'

'Let's say we were both at fault.'

His arms released her completely and she stepped away from him, swaying slightly. At once he caught hold of her again.

'I haven't hurt you?' he asked anxiously. 'You're so little that I——'

'I'm fine,' she interrupted. 'It's just that I've never been kissed like this before.'

He gave an abrupt laugh, but it held no vestige of sarcasm. 'You're very innocent, Abby. If it will make you feel better, you may smack my face.'

'Then we'd be back to square one, and that would be pointless and humiliating.'

Less shaky now, she was able to move away from him, and went over to the table where she picked up her unfinished copy of the miniature.

'Leave it where it is,' he ordered. 'I'll see that no one touches it. Then it will be ready for you to go on working on it tomorrow.'

'Thank you.'

'But I suggest you do it during the day. You'll find it less tiring on your eyes.'

'During the day I'm with your aunt,' she pointed out.

'Do you enjoy working for her?' he asked.

'We're hardly working yet. I'm more of a companion than anything else.'

'She'll have your nose to the grindstone once you get back to England,' he said, and ran his hand over his hair to smooth it down. The front was ruffled, as if she had raked it with her fingers, but she had no memory of having done so, and quickly averted her eyes from him.

'Abby,' he said, 'I want to apologise again for——'

'It isn't necessary,' she interrupted him. 'Or are you worried that I'll tell your aunt what happened tonight?'

'She'd probably be delighted if you did.'

Face flaming, Abby glared at him. Amusement crinkled the corners of his mouth and he looked almost gentle.

'All the more reason for me not to tell her,' Abby said aloud, and went to the door. Her hand was on the knob when he spoke again.

'You're partly to blame for what happened, Abby. During these past few weeks you've done your best to get under my skin.'

'I've done the exact opposite,' she flared. 'I've done my best to keep out of your way.'

'I've never known anyone make themselves so obvious by their absence.'

'That wasn't my intention.'

'Possibly not. But it's what happened.'

'Then you should blame your own guilty conscience,' she said boldly. 'That's what made you aware that I was avoiding you. If you hadn't known that you'd behaved badly, you wouldn't have noticed what I was doing.'

He gave the slightest of smiles. 'Please don't avoid me in future. It isn't necessary.'

'Very well,' she said, without any intention of taking notice of him. 'Goodnight, Mr Farrow.'

'You'd better make it Giles; it's more civilised.'

Wandering around her bedroom—there was no point trying to go to sleep, for she was too overwrought—Abby thought of the scene that had taken place between them and wondered if it had been a dream. But her lips, still hurting from his brutal kiss, told her it had been a reality, and she knew her awareness of him would be intensified. The knowledge frightened her and she wished there was some way of maintaining a neutral attitude to him. She did not want to go on disliking him, yet equally important, she definitely did not want to like him. To do so could be dangerous.

Refusing to think why this might be so, she went over to the window to adjust the curtains. In the garden she saw a dark form move away from a clump of trees and recognised Giles Farrow pacing the narrow path that skirted the pool. So he was also too restless to sleep. She saw the pale blur of his face as he raised his head to the sky, and his profile glowed in the small flame of a lighter as he lit a cigar. Then darkness enveloped him again and with a sigh she twitched the curtains together and went to bed.

She awoke to the cool light of an Indian dawn and, staring out at the pinkish grey sky, thought immediately of Giles Farrow. She still found it difficult to know why he had kissed her. Anger to begin with, of course, but afterwards, when the anger had died, he had not reverted to his usual sardonic self but had spoken to her as if he were seeing her for the first time, and did not dislike what he saw.

Too restless to remain in bed, she showered and dressed and went down to the garden. As always there was a slight breeze, and the air had the fresh tang of the sea about it so that she breathed in deeply, filled with an unexpected joy that came from she knew not where. She pirouetted lightly across the grass—a slip of a girl with long, honey-gold hair and large pansy-brown eyes, delighting in the softness of the earth and the blueness of the sky.

At eight o'clock she was sitting on the terrace having

her breakfast. The marmalade and toast were delicious, but she still avoided taking any butter, which was of such poor quality that it was not worth eating. It tasted more like solidified ghee, the clarified butter in which Indians did their cooking but which bore no relation in taste or look to European butter. But the excellence of the fruit more than made up for this, and there was a profusion of choice from enormous tangerines, apples, mangoes and small, delicious-tasting bananas, each one no bigger than a man's index finger.

She was just finishing a third cup of coffee when Giles Farrow came out on to the terrace. He had never appeared at breakfast before and she wondered if this was a new departure for him or whether he was taking a day off.

'You're up early,' he commented.

'I still can't get used to the perfect weather and it seems a pity to waste it by staying in my room.'

'Do you usually dance around the lawn to greet the day?'

Her cup wobbled in her hand, but she spoke coolly. 'If I'm happy I always dance—sometimes I sing too.'

His mouth quirked. 'Is there any particular reason for your happiness this morning?'

'Perhaps because we're friends,' she said gravely. 'Not real friends, but at least we're no longer enemies.'

'And that made you happy enough to dance?'

'Yes.' She sighed. 'It isn't pleasant to stay in a house when you're not wanted.'

He was silent, frowning, his well-shaped brows almost meeting above his long straight nose. 'I hadn't realised you found my behaviour so upsetting,' he said finally. 'You always gave me the impression that you didn't care a jot what I thought of you.' His glance was penetrating as it rested on her. 'For someone who seems so transparent, you hide your feelings very well.'

'That's not a logical comment, coming from you, Mr Farrow.'

'Giles,' he reminded her.

She went pink and then nodded. 'If I'm transparent, how can I hide my feelings? I think you should reassess your opinion of me. Either I'm not transparent—in which case you can't see through me and guess my motivation—or I *am* transparent and you'll always be able to *know* what I feel!'

Unexpectedly he laughed, and the moment lessened the severity of his features. His face was alive with warmth and his eyes glowed with humour. As always, she was fascinated by their ability to go from amber to gold and then to darkest topaz. Aware that she was staring at him, she pushed back her chair.

'Please don't rush off,' he said. 'We declared a pact last night, if you remember.'

Abby subsided again, her hands suddenly clammy. To have Giles Farrow friendly to her was almost as disconcerting as having him antagonistic. She searched for something to say, but could think of nothing bright or witty. He did not seem to mind her silence, but went on carefully peeling an apple. He had beautifully shaped hands for a man, the fingers long and the nails oval. She recollected their touch on her skin and quickly focused on less intimate thoughts.

'Did you always want to be a nuclear engineer?' she asked at random, saying the first thing that came into her head.

If he was surprised by the question, he did not show it. 'I first wanted to be a train driver,' he smiled, and began to cut his apple into sections.

'But after you got over *that* particular ambition?'

'I then decided to follow my father. He'd been in the same profession. My interest in nuclear physics grew from that.'

'And now you're one of the top men in your field. You must feel very proud.'

'I suppose I do,' he said, after a moment's thought. 'But it tends to make you spoilt. Everyone defers to your opinions and you expect that to happen in your private life too.'

She wondered if he was thinking of his broken engagement and regretting the stand he had taken. But she dared not ask him, and when next he spoke it was to change the subject completely.

'Tell me about your own background, Abby,' he asked.

'It was a very ordinary one. My father died when I was a child and my mother worked terribly hard to support us. I left school as soon as I could, but even with my wages coming in, things weren't easy. But then my twin sisters were discovered in a beauty contest and from then on things got better.'

'They're models now, aren't they? My aunt mentioned something about it.'

'Very famous models,' said Abby. 'You've probably seen them without realising it. They were the twins in the big whisky campaign last year.'

His expression told her that a visual image had flashed in front of him.

'Those two girls are your sisters?' he asked in astonishment.

'I'm the plain one of the family,' she said bluntly.

He reached out for another apple and she was illogically disappointed that he made no comment. Still, what could he have said that would have been flattering to her? She bit back a sigh and was glad when a step behind her announced the arrival of Miss Bateman.

'Come on, Abby, we're going shopping,' she announced. 'I'm tired of working.'

'Then let me do some typing for you,' Abby pleaded. 'My holiday has gone on long enough.'

'Just listen to the child pleading to work!' Miss Bateman regarded her nephew. 'She's incredible, isn't she? But I've made up my mind. I want to do some shopping and I refuse to go alone.'

'I'll fetch my handbag and meet you at the car.'

Smiling briefly at Giles, Abby hurried away. She was glad their conversation had been interrupted. Although their enmity had ended, she didn't want friendship to take its place. For friendship from Giles might grow into something that would be far more destructive to her peace of mind than his enmity had been.

CHAPTER TEN

MISS BATEMAN did her shopping the way she did everything—with unbounded enthusiasm—and the car was soon laden with brass bowls, leather bags, and sari lengths of brocade and pure silk.

By eleven-thirty Abby was prepared to call it a day and return to the house, but her employer had still only completed half her shopping, seemingly intent on buying gifts for every one of her numerous friends.

'I'd like to buy you a little something too,' she said, but Abby, knowing that the woman's 'little something' could turn out to be something far from little, firmly refused the offer.

It was one-thirty before they finally reached the resplendent Taj Mahal hotel, where Miss Bateman had decided they were to have lunch.

'You've seen so little of Bombay that I feel guilty about it,' she explained, and led the way into an enormous square marble foyer, predominantly decorated in gold and white.

In London, Abby had had occasion to visit most of the luxurious West End hotels to make special deliveries of one or other valuable book to a customer, but she could not remember seeing a foyer as busy as this one. And the diversity of the people in it! Arabs in flowing white robes; Chinese in stark black jackets and narrow trousers; Savile Row-suited Englishmen and the casual attire of the Australian and American. All the world and his wife—and probably his mistress too

—seemed to be milling round the vast length of the reception desk, where a dozen or more clerks were handing out keys from a board which looked as complex as a computer.

Miss Bateman led the way across the foyer and turned left down an arcade lined with shops as elegant as one would find in the Burlington Arcade. She had only taken a few paces when a tall, slim girl emerged from one of the shops and almost bumped into them.

'Hello, Vicky,' Miss Bateman sounded distinctly unenthusiastic. 'I didn't expect to see you here. Giles told me you were flying up to spend a few days at the Bird Sanctuary.'

'Jack went alone. I couldn't face the prospect of sitting quiet as a mouse for hours at a time watching my little feathered friends.'

Vicky looked at the diamond watch on her wrist, as if to indicate a pressing appointment, and Miss Bateman nodded curtly and stalked on. Abby followed, carrying a vivid picture of Vicky in her mind. How stunning she had looked in a vivid pink dress and jacket that had drawn attention to her exotic dark looks. Abby felt as dowdy as a pigeon by comparison and wished she too could make male heads turn. But not all male heads. Only one.

'Here we are.'

Miss Bateman stopped outside a heavy wood door bearing the name Dragon Room. Predictably it proved to be a Chinese restaurant, filled to overflowing, though a table was found for them as soon as she gave her name.

Abby was surprised they should be eating Chinese food in India, but understood why when the meal—which her employer knowledgeably ordered—was set before them, for it was the most delicious she had tasted, bearing as much relation to the Chinese food she had eaten in London as dogs did to cats.

'One can't drink wine with this type of meal,' Miss Bateman said. 'So how about champagne?'

Abby laughed. 'Isn't that wine too?'

'Yes, but sparkling, so it goes with food. But if you'd prefer ordinary wine . . .'

'I'd prefer China tea,' Abby said firmly.

'Saving my money for me?' came the dry response. 'You needn't, my dear. I have far more than I could ever spend in two lifetimes. If Giles doesn't hurry and give me a few great-nephews and nieces to spoil, I'll have to build a gold-plated cats' home!'

Abby laughed again, and tried not to think of Giles' children. But it was all too easy to visualise them: sturdy little youngsters, tall and straight-backed the way he was, with the same brown hair and amber eyes. Determinedly she concentrated on her food, angry for once more letting this unpredictable man take over her thoughts.

Lunch over, Miss Bateman rested in the garden room at the far end of the arcade, while Abby set off to explore the rest of the hotel.

It was like a world of its own, with half a dozen restaurants, many different shopping areas apart from the large main one, and patios where guests could sit and watch exotic birds and fish. She was amused by the American-style coffee bar, which seemed so incongruous filled with sari-clad ladies, and infinitely preferred the Tandoori, a dimly lit Indian restaurant where one of the waiters, seeing her peep in enquiringly, was happy to show her around, most of the clients having already departed.

'I hope you will come and have lunch or dinner here one day,' he said. 'We do an excellent Tandoori chicken. It is very special.'

'I had it once in London,' Abby told him.

'It couldn't have been as good as you will get here. It must be cooked in a brick oven. Please follow me and I will show you ours.'

He led her across the restaurant, which was set on raised tiers, and then through to the kitchen which was modern, exceptionally clean, and hot as Hades. What it was like in the summer, when the temperature outside was over a hundred degrees, Abby dared not think.

'There you are.' Her escort pointed to a large brick-built oven, heated by coal and attended by a dark-skinned Indian who, at a muttered order, opened the oven door, which immediately sent out a terrific blast of heat and a glimpse of scarlet-coloured poultry.

'It smells delicious,' Abby gasped, and fell back a step. 'I'll definitely order it when I come here.'

Satisfied that he had gained a convert, the waiter led her back through the restaurant again, and she was nearly by the exit when she saw the man and woman sitting at a table some few yards to her left. They were too engrossed in one another to notice her, but even in the dim lighting the pink silk dress was recognisable, as was the man's mahogany brown hair and classical features. So that was why Vicky had elected to remain behind in Bombay! Anger and disgust welled up in her. How could Giles be so stupid as to still want the woman who had let him down so badly many years ago and who, by seeing him now, was also letting down her husband?

Quickly Abby walked down the steps, averting her head as she came nearer the table. But she need not have bothered; neither the man nor the woman were paying any attention to anyone around them. Resolutely she returned to Miss Bateman.

'I didn't expect you back so soon,' the woman said. 'I hope you didn't rush on my account.'

Abby shook her head. 'I've seen all I want.'

How true that was! she thought wryly, and wished that the image of Giles and his lady love could be expunged from her mind. Why did Vicky Laughton want to see him again? Was it to prove she still had a hold over him, or was it just an innocuous meeting of erstwhile lovers who were now merely good friends? Somehow Abby could not see such a woman being friends with anyone, particularly a handsome man.

'You're very quiet,' Miss Bateman commented. 'Is anything the matter?'

'I have a slight headache,' Abby lied, and followed her employer out to the car.

Unseeingly she stared at the passing street, with its taxis and bikes and the inevitable beggars who tapped at the windows as they were halted by the many traffic jams.

Why should I care that I've seen Giles Farrow lunching with Vicky Laughton? she asked herself in quiet desperation. It's his life and he can do what he likes with it; it makes no difference to me! But that was a lie, and even as she thought it, she had to admit it as such. It *did* make a difference to her. With every nerve in her body she wanted to be in Vicky Laughton's place. She wanted Giles Farrow to look at her in the same hungry way. Without realising it she must have given a gasp, for Miss Bateman put her hand on her arm and looked at her with concern.

'Are you sure you're all right, my dear? I didn't make you eat too much, did I?'

'It's only a bit of indigestion,' Abby replied, offering the excuse given her.

'I'll order some lemon and sugar for you as soon as we get home. It's a wonderful tummy settler.'

The car accelerated as they climbed Malibar Hill with the large houses and the apartment blocks set back in gardens and surrounded by trees. They entered their own drive and came to a stop.

'If you don't want me for anything special,' Abby said quickly, 'I'd like to lie down for a while.'

'Of course. Stay in your room as long as you like,' Miss Bateman said. 'I have masses of notes to make.'

Gratefully Abby hurried away. She had to be by herself; to assimilate the knowledge she had just learned and to see if thinking about it again would help it to disappear. With a deep sense of the inevitable she knew this would not be the case. For better or for worse she was in love.

How had it happened and when? Only a short time ago she had not even liked him! It's purely sexual attraction, she told herself. It couldn't be anything more meaningful, for they had nothing in common. Yet sexual attraction, while it lasted—and it could last for a very long time—had the power to hurt. If this weren't the case, she wouldn't have been so shattered to see the way Giles had looked into Vicky Laughton's beautiful face this afternoon.

'How can he let her make a fool of him all over again?' she muttered as she slammed the bedroom door behind her. But then men in love were easily turned into fools—as were women!—and in this respect Giles was no worse than the rest of men.

Going down to dinner later that evening, she was dismayed to find Giles was dining at home. He looked particularly handsome in a honeysuckle silk sweater and tan slacks. His casual attire made him seem younger too, and it was harder for her to see him as the intellectually brilliant man who held such onerous responsibility.

'You're looking very solemn,' he commented, as she walked towards him.

She shrugged without answering and, after another sharp look at her, he came to her side with a drink.

'I don't want anything, thanks,' she told him.

'Try it. It's only fruit juice.'

Reluctantly she took the glass and sipped from it. Out of the corner of her eye she saw him watching her and wished she were not so affected by his nearness. She moved towards Miss Bateman, afraid that if she remained by his side he would see she was trembling.

'I've just been telling Giles that I want to go on a little trip,' the woman said. Abby looked at her blankly, her mind still on the man behind her. 'To Aurangabad,' Miss Bateman continued. 'It's an hour's flight from here.'

With an effort Abby tried to remember what she had read about it. 'Isn't it famous for its caves?' she murmured.

'It's *only* famous for its cave,' was the amused answer. 'Aurangabad itself is nothing more than a village with a few hotels built to cater for the tourists who only go there to see the cave and the rock temples.'

Abby nodded, full memory returning as she did so. The Temples of Ajanta, discovered in 1819 in a crescent-shaped ravine some fifty miles from the town of Aurangabad, were a supreme example of early art, having been painted some two hundred years before the birth of Christ.

'If it's convenient for you,' Miss Bateman said, 'I'd

like to go there the day after tomorrow. Giles will arrange the tickets for us.'

'I may not be able to get them,' he interposed. 'You know the state of chaos of the Internal Service.'

'I have no doubts about you getting them,' his aunt said firmly. 'The Government will do anything if you ask them.'

'You rate me too highly,' he smiled.

'I know your worth,' she replied. 'And it's time you acknowledged it too.'

Aunt and nephew eyed each other as though crossing mental swords, and Abby had the presentiment that Miss Bateman knew he had been lunching with his ex-fiancée.

'Why don't you come with us to Aurangabad?' Miss Bateman suggested.

'I'm not sure I can get away.'

'Is it work that keeps you?'

'What else?' he said blandly. 'I'll see if I can arrange it. It might be an idea to get away from Bombay for a few days.'

To hide her face, Abby turned quickly and placed her glass on the sideboard. But Giles immediately joined her, placing his own glass beside hers and blocking her escape by standing directly in front of her.

'Why didn't you say hello to me when you saw me in the restaurant this afternoon?' he asked.

If it was his intention to surprise her, he succeeded, for she stared at him speechlessly.

'I know you saw me,' he added.

'I didn't know you saw *me*.'

'I'm not blind.' His eyes glinted. 'Did you ignore me because you didn't approve of me being with Vicky?'

'It isn't my business to judge you.'

'I've yet to know that to stop a woman!' His head tilted towards her. 'Tell me, is that why you didn't come over?'

'Certainly not. I didn't think you wanted me to.'

He still remained close, but his eyebrows had lowered and the shadow of them darkened his eyes and made their expression difficult to fathom.

'Did you tell my aunt you saw me?' he asked.

'No. I wouldn't want to disappoint her.'

He caught his breath. 'You choose your words well.'

'I wish I could say the same about the way you choose your women.'

She was sorry the instant she had spoken, fearing that her retort had given away her true feelings. But she need not have worried. Giles was too irritated by the face value of her comment to realise it might have any deeper implication.

'You are in no position to judge Vicky,' he said slowly. 'Love isn't the way you read in fairy tales, where everyone does the right thing and lives happily ever after. In real life people make mistakes and pay for them.'

'Are you talking about yourself too?' Abby asked coolly.

'Does the answer matter to you?'

'Not particularly. Your emotions are your own affair.'

'I thought we were friends,' he said quietly, 'and friends don't judge each other without first knowing the facts of the situation.'

'You didn't really believe we're friends,' Abby said, half turning away from him. 'I'm sure that what I think of you and Mrs Laughton can be of no importance to you.'

'You underestimate yourself,' he said drily.

'What are you two whispering about?' Miss Bateman called across the room.

'The political situation,' her nephew replied promptly.

'You'll never be able to solve it,' said Miss Bateman.

'All problems can be solved given the will to do so,' Giles replied.

There was a spark of mischief in the amber eyes, but Abby refused to be appeased by it and, unsmilingly, went to sit on one of the settees. She was surprised that Giles had been curious to know why she had avoided him in the restaurant and decided it had been his way of finding out it she had mentioned it to his aunt. Resolutely she kept her eyes on the carpet, trying to ignore the fact that Giles had come to sit beside her, one leg crossed over the other, his foot swinging idly. She hoped he was not going to accompany them to Aurangabad. The idea of spending several days in his company was too painful to contemplate and she wondered if there was any way she could avoid going if he really had decided to join them.

'What are you thinking?' he asked softly.

'Why you wanted to go to Aurangabad,' she answered promptly. 'I'm sure you've already seen it.'

'I have. But it's worth another look. Besides, I need to get away and I'm sure your busy little mind can come up with any number of sordid reasons.'

'Only one,' she retorted. 'Running from temptation.'

The look he gave her was deliberately insolent. 'How do you know I'm not running *into* it?'

She felt colour come into her cheeks, and the blush was not lessened by his amused chuckle.

'If you're going to fight me, Abby, don't use words,' he said.

'What else can I use?'

Slowly his eyes moved from the top of her soft, straight hair down her slender body to her small feet neatly crossed at the ankles. 'You have an armoury of far more subtle weapons, Abby West, but you're too innocent to know how to use them.'

'It's an innocence I prefer to retain,' she snapped.

'That's a pity. Ripe fruit is meant to be eaten; it should never be allowed to wither on the bough.'

There was absolutely nothing she could say to this and she acknowledged defeat with a faint sigh. Giles was right when he said she should not cross verbal swords with him. He was a sophisticate who could run rings around her without even trying. And tonight, for reasons best known to himself, he was baiting her and flirting with her. Not for one moment did she believe it was because he genuinely found her attractive. Maybe it was his way of showing her that emotion could make fools of everyone.

A servant came in to say that dinner was served and she jumped to her feet and was at the door before anyone else had risen.

'You must be hungry,' Giles drawled with amusement.

'I could eat a horse,' she retorted.

'That's better than eating a man,' he replied, and blandly gave his aunt his arm to lead her in to dinner.

CHAPTER ELEVEN

GILES did not go to his office the following day but spent half the morning arranging their trip to Aurangabad and the other half in a lengthy discussion with his aunt about some of her investments.

Reluctant to listen in to what was obviously a family matter, Abby sat on the other side of the swimming pool. She did not venture into the water, having a strange reluctance to wear her bikini in Giles' presence. Instead she was content to remain in her sun-dress, and when it became too hot, moved beneath the shade of a large parasol.

Miss Bateman had still refused to let her start typing back the cassette into which she was dictating her latest thriller, but Abby had taken one of her employer's copious notebooks and was reading the scrawled longhand with the intention of typing all the notes back in a more readable form. She was engrossed on a particularly indecipherable word when a shadow fell across her head. and she knew without needing to look up that it belonged to Giles.

'Why don't you go in for a swim?' he asked, dropping down on to the deck chair beside her.

She kept her eyes low on the page but nonetheless glimpsed bare, deeply tanned legs.

'Or would you prefer to go to the beach?' he went on. 'Juhu is worth a visit.'

'Why are you being so friendly?' she asked.

'Didn't we declare pax a couple of nights ago? Or

would you prefer to go back to being enemies?' He gave an unexpected sigh. 'I'm surprised you're so narrow-minded, Abby.'

'Narrow-minded? Me?'

'Very much so. Seeing me with Vicky has ruffled your fur and you've been decidedly snappy ever since.'

'I'm an old-fashioned girl,' she said evenly, 'and I don't like deceit.'

'Vicky and I were once engaged,' he said quietly. 'It would be foolish to pretend we'd never known each other. Besides, it's a good thing to be able to look back on the past without regret.'

'Other people might not find that so easy to believe,' she said. 'Mr Laughton wouldn't feel complacent about the two of you meeting each other. In similar circumstances, I wouldn't.'

'Don't tell me you'd be jealous of your husband?'

'I certainly would if I saw him having a tête-à-tête with a girl he'd once promised to marry. Particularly if he hadn't been the one to break the engagement in the first place.'

'Well, well,' Giles taunted, 'I'm delighted to hear you're capable of jealousy. At least it shows you have deeper feelings than I realised.'

'You're not in a position to realise anything about my feelings,' she snapped, and was about to jump to her feet when his arms came across her chair and restrained her.

'You're always making innuendoes, and then running away,' he said softly. 'But I won't let you this time.'

Recognising the futility of trying to escape, she leaned back against the canvas. 'Let me go, Giles. I'm sure the depth of my emotion doesn't matter to you one way or the other.'

'But it does,' he replied. 'You're such an elusive little thing that I never thought I'd notice if you were here or not. But funnily enough I do. You're not a violent rain storm, Abby—one can see it coming and protect oneself against that. You're a gentle drizzle that soaks you through to the skin before you realise it.'

'How nice.' She tried to keep her voice humorous. 'I love being compared with drizzle!'

'So you should. There's nothing nicer than walking in soft gentle rain.'

'It can give you the death of a cold,' she retorted.

'But what a lovely way to die!'

Before she could thing of a suitable retort, he rose and sauntered over to the deep end of the pool. He stood there for a moment looking at the water, his body bare except for the tight, revealing swimming shorts. As she watched, he dived cleanly into the water and swam steadily beneath the surface, only coming up for air as he reached the opposite end. He paused there briefly and then swam back and heaved himself up on the side.

'Don't be a coward, Abby,' he chided. 'Come in for a swim.'

She knew that if she refused he would see it as a sign of her embarrassment, and she unbuttoned her sun-dress and stepped out of it. Though small, her limbs were beautifully rounded, and conscious of Giles subjecting her to an intensive scrutiny, she went to the opposite end of the pool and jumped feet first into the water. It was not the most glamorous way of getting in, but she could not dive and had no intention of going in inch by trembling inch. Shaking the water out of her eyes, she surfaced and then did a brisk crawl across the pool, to finish up where Giles' feet were dangling into the water.

'It was a lousy way to get in, for an excellent swimmer,' he quipped. 'Have you never been taught how to dive?'

'No.'

'Like me to teach you?'

It was an unexpected offer and she found herself nodding before she had a chance to think about it. Then there was no more chance to think, for he stood up, stretched out his hand and hoisted her out of the water.

'Now then, stand close to the edge and put your feet together. Then bend slightly at the knees and relax your body.'

For the next hour he patiently and carefully took her through the basics of a simple dive, making her repeat it again and again until she started to do it automatically. She had judged him to be a quick-tempered man and was agreeably surprised to find that no matter how frequently she made mistakes, he would gently show her how to cure them. He was tireless, and would have continued his instruction if his aunt had not marched over and ordered him to stop.

'The child is puffing like a whale,' she protested, at which remark he turned and subjected Abby to a close stare.

Immediately she became conscious of her shallow breathing and the quick rise and fall of her breasts, and made an effort to breathe slowly.

'You should have stopped me earlier,' he said apologetically, and put his arms around her shoulders.

She went rigid in his hold and he let her go at once, the friendliness evaporating from his face. Knowing she had been childish and regretting her lack of control, she returned to her chair for her sun-dress, and was picking it up when Giles was beside her again.

'Use this,' he said, draping a short bathrobe around her. 'Keep up your guard, little fruit,' he added quietly, 'or before you know it, you'll be falling from the bough!'

Colour high, she gripped the towelling robe close, caught up her dress and went quickly into the house.

She took her time about changing and coming downstairs again, but she need not have worried, for Giles had gone out and did not return until midway through the afternoon. He was formally dressed in a cream tropical suit, and she could not help a flash of jealousy as she wondered if he had been lunching with Vicky Laughton again. From the gleam in his eyes as they met her own, she knew he had guessed her thoughts, but he merely gave her a mocking smile.

'Our flight has been confirmed for tomorrow,' he informed his aunt, 'but I'm afraid it's an early one. The plane leaves at seven-thirty and it means we must leave here promptly at five-thirty.'

'So early?' Abby questioned.

'It's a long run to the airport and we have to be there a full hour before take-off. If we arrive a minute late we may find there's a good chance that our tickets will have been given to people on stand-by.'

'What sort of clothes should I take?' she asked.

'Cotton dresses and your most comfortable shoes. We're flying south, so it will be pretty hot.'

He ran a finger around his shirt collar, surprising her by the gesture, for he looked extremely cool. Yet a second glance showed a flush of colour on his cheekbones and a faint film of perspiration above his upper lip. She longed to touch it with her hand and to rest her head on the curve of his throat. It was a treacherous feeling that frightened her to her feet and made her murmur that she was going in search of a book.

But even in the library, away from his presence, she was still aware of him. It made her understand the many things her highly susceptible twin sisters used to say, for they fell in and out of love with monotonous regularity; unlike herself who, until now, had never experienced such a feeling. But this did not mean she would never experience it again for another man. Giles was the first one to arouse her sexually but it was foolish to think he would be the last. One day another man would come into her life who would arouse the same feeling but who, unlike this enigmatic one, would respond with love as well as with passion.

Footsteps sounded on the marble floor and she hurriedly turned to the bookcase and took the first book that came to hand. She was holding it against her as Giles came in.

'You'll find it quite safe to rejoin my aunt,' he said. 'I'm going out.'

Her head lifted. 'I wasn't running away from you.'

'Weren't you?'

Before she knew what he intended to do, he strode over and plucked the book from her hand. He glanced at it and his eyebrows rose.

'*The Political, Social & Economic Problems of India.* That's a nice bit of light reading,' he commented. 'Just the thing for hot afternoons.'

She snatched the book away from him and replaced it on the shelf. She heard him chuckle.

'At least you're being honest, Abby. Choose something else.'

'All right,' she said bluntly. 'I did come in here to get out of your way. But can't you understand why? I'm uncomfortable when you're around. You embarrass me and make me nervous.'

'I don't do it intentionally,' he protested.

'You make fun of me all the time.' She forced herself to face him. 'Stop baiting me, Giles. It's cruel, not clever.'

'Cruel?' he echoed, the smile leaving his face. 'I've never wanted to be cruel—not since I began to understand you. But I'm beginning to see I've been exceptionally stupid.'

'What do you mean?' she asked.

There was a long pause before he spoke. 'I won't answer that question, Abby. I'd prefer to wait until you're able to answer it for yourself.'

She was still trying to work out what this meant when he left the room, moving with ill-concealed impatience.

True to his word, she did not see Giles again that day, and when she came down into the hall promptly at five-thirty the next morning, he was already there, supervising the cases as they were carried to the car.

The skies had not lightened, yet it was almost as warm and sultry as it was during the day, with not a breath of air to stir the leaves.

'My aunt's already in the car,' said Giles, and Abby went outside and climbed in beside Miss Bateman. Giles sat in front beside the chauffeur and they set off.

It was a pleasure to drive through the streets at this hour. There was hardly any traffic, so there was no necessity to constantly hoot on the horn to warn jaywalkers and cyclists. But despite the speed they managed, it was still a lengthy journey to the airport, and when they arrived, hundreds of people were milling round everywhere, with crowds in front of the Air India stand and piles of luggage making progress difficult. While Abby and Miss Bateman stood to one side, Giles proceeded to get their tickets and luggage cleared with a maximum of efficiency that made him seem an oasis of calm in this hurly-burly. Looking at him, one could not doubt his nationality, for he exuded British phlegm.

Promptly at seven-thirty they boarded the twin-engined turbo-prop for an hour's flight in perfect weather, and landed in what appeared to be the middle of a desert marked only by a single-storied airport building.

Moments later they were speeding along a dirt road, with flat scrubland stretching interminably on either side of them. Looking for the village of Aurangabad, Abby was surprised when she suddenly saw two modern hotels within a hundred yards of one another, standing up starkly in this arid land. They drove past the first, but turned off into the drive of the second, being saluted by an armed guard as they did so.

'Where's the village?' she asked.

'A few miles further down the road,' Miss Bateman answered. 'When I was last here, these hotels weren't even built, and we had to stay in very primitive huts.'

'Now it's all modern conveniences for the tourists,' Giles added, 'with ice water in the dining-room and face tissues in the bathroom.'

'What's wrong with a few comforts?' said Abby, and knew from his smile that he was teasing her again.

Despite the bleakness by which it was surrounded, the hotel was perfectly appointed, with comfortable furniture, excellent decor and willing staff. After a quickly satisfying breakfast, they took a leisurely drive round Aurangabad, seeing the colourful market where the inevitable cows wandered aimlessly, eating the refuse in an effort to keep alive.

They returned to the hotel for lunch and then drove

out through cotton fields and gently rolling hills to the starker outcrop of Ellora. It was here, in these higher rocky mountains, that thirty-four temples had been dug, some of them Hindu and the rest Buddhist and Jain.

Some two thousand tons of stones had been removed by hand as masons had carved slowly, inch by inch, deep into the bowels of the hills. Abby found it incredible that these constructions had been worked from the top downwards, and her admiration intensified at the sight of the richly decorated interiors and façades. For some reason best known to themselves, the masons had reproduced the timber roofs of their day, making the stone look amazingly like wood. Over the course of the years the weather had taken its toll and many of the magnificently carved mythological animals and tall columns had crumbled. But their remains were left as a testimony to the passing of time, which increased the feeling of great age and made one even more appreciative of those which remained.

Miss Bateman was an indefatigable sightseer, and marched resolutely up and down the steps as she went from one temple to another. Abby was tired after she had only seen a quarter of what was available, and contentedly sat on some steps and lifted her face to the sun.

'Aren't you impressed by all this?'

Giles' voice made her open her eyes, and she saw him looking down at her with amusement. His hands were thrust into the pockets of his trousers and his sports shirt was opened at the neck. In the sunshine his hair was more noticeably mahogany, and the redness of it gave him an unusually devilish appearance.

'One temple is much like another to me,' she said. 'I could look at paintings for hours on end, but this

sort of rock carving and sculpture doesn't move me. I
suppose that makes me a philistine in your eyes?'

'I'd consider you more of a philistine if you'd pretended to like something you didn't. The one thing I've
come to expect from you, Abby, in the short time I've
known you, is honesty.'

'Even to the point of rudeness?'

He gave a wide, disarming smile. 'On this lovely
warm afternoon I wouldn't even object to your rudeness.'

They were words she was to remember not long
afterwards, but since she was not clairvoyant, she accepted them now with gratification. She stood up,
knowing he was waiting for her to follow him to yet
another cave temple. Though she had professed herself
to be unmoved by the sculpture depicted here, this
particular shrine was so beautifully carved with gods
and animals that she was overwhelmed by them, more
so when she realised the enormous human effort it had
taken to fashion them out of the black, organic rock
hillside.

'How did the stone workers know what they were
doing?' she asked. 'I mean, it's hard enough to carve
a rock when you're looking at it face on. But if you're
working from the top and digging down ...'

'I think they dug a deep trench all the way round a
given piece of rock. Then they clambered down to the
bottom of it and started to hack away.'

'It must have been some trench,' she muttered. 'A
hundred feet deep at least.'

'That's what makes it so incredible. And we think
we've got craftsmen today.' He waved his hand. 'The
majesty of this just leaves us standing.'

She knew exactly what he meant, and sharing his

opinion made her feel closer to him. It also made her realise how little she knew of his feeling and opinions, and she wondered what he had been like as a younger man and a child. Had he always possessed the same quality of elusiveness which he had today?

'What have you decided?' he asked abruptly.

'About what?'

'About me. For the last few minutes you've looked as if you've been measuring me up.'

The expression made her smile. 'I was wondering what you were like as a child and if you were always so self-possessed.'

'Is that how you see me?' He did not wait for her answer. 'As a kid I was a difficult combination—clever, shy and exceptionally determined. I was devoted to my father—he was a fantastic man, an engineer and a poet and I wanted to be like him.'

'Did you write poetry too?'

'I still do.' His eyes narrowed, making Abby feel he was assessing her yet again. 'One day I'll show some to you.'

'One day?'

'You're not ready for it yet.'

Annoyed by the implication that he still regarded her as emotionally immature, she walked away from him. As far as he was concerned, she was his aunt's companion and secretary, a naïve young woman whom he had misjudged at their first meeting and whom he was now trying to put at ease—though his way of doing so made her feel like a not particularly bright teenager. It had been foolish of her to imagine he had come to Aurangabad because he enjoyed her company. He had come because he wanted to escape from Bombay; to put some distance between himself and Vicky Laughton. This thought brightened her mood, for it meant he was trying his best not to succumb to his feelings for another man's wife.

'How about a cool drink?' Giles asked, and without waiting for her reply, put a firm hand under her elbow and guided her over the uneven stones into the full force of the afternoon's sun. Their car was parked some twenty yards away, in the shade of a group of straggly trees, and he led her towards it.

'Don't tell me there's a café around here?' she asked.

'I won't,' he smiled, and opening the boot, took out a canvas holdall from which he extracted a thermos flask and a couple of glasses. Deftly he poured iced fruit juice into them and handed her one.

'Do you always come prepared for everything?' she asked admiringly.

'I'm a seasoned traveller.'

'I don't think you're at a loss, whatever you do.'

'You sound as if you find that rather worrying,' he commented.

'It could be,' she said solemnly. 'It's hard to live up to perfection.'

'I'm glad you see me as perfect!'

How awful if he were to guess she had fallen in love with him.

'Where's Miss Bateman?' she asked jerkily.

'Taking pictures of one of the shrines. The driver is with her, so she'll be perfectly all right.'

'You worry about her, don't you?'

'Yes. She's a game old lady, but she *is* old. I'm glad you were with her when she was ill.'

Abby was warmed by the compliment. 'Then you've no longer got any worries about my taking advantage of her?'

He frowned. 'Don't remind me of the things I once said to you. I could kick myself.'

She smiled and sipped her drink. Giles did the same, his expression so enigmatic that she longed to know what was in his mind.

'It's time I gave you a penny for your thoughts,' she said.

'I was trying to see myself from your point of view,' he confessed. 'I'm not sure I like what I saw.'

'You don't know how I feel,' she protested.

'Don't I? I could make a good guess.' He began to enumerate. 'You've already said I'm aloof and unfriendly. You've said I'm perfect and would expect others to be perfect too, which implies that I'm smug and lack understanding.'

'Oh no! You're being far too harsh on yourself. I don't see you that way at all.'

'Then how do you see me?'

'One day I might tell you,' she prevaricated, then added: 'Two can play at the same game, Giles.'

For an instant he looked surprised, then he chuckled.

'You may be five foot nothing, Abby West, but you're all tongue!'

Unexpectedly he caught her hand and squeezed it, and he was still holding it when his aunt descended upon them, dabbing at her face with a large, man-sized handkerchief. Gratefully she accepted the cold drink her nephew proffered.

'A bath and bed for me,' she announced as they climbed into the car and headed for the hotel. 'You two young things will have to entertain each other tonight.'

Abby half opened her mouth to say she would also remain in her room, and then decided against it. If she continued to avoid being alone with Giles he would certainly suspect her motives.

'I'm afraid I can't offer to hit the high spots with you, Abby,' he said. 'The night life of Aurangabad is as dull as its daylight!'

She giggled. 'After traipsing around those shrines I'll be more than happy to sit and sit!'

'Good. I'll be in the bar at eight o'clock. Meet me there when you're ready.'

Looking through her meagre wardrobe after she had showered, Abby wished she had packed something more glamorous than the simple cottons Giles had suggested. Yet even if she had brought something eye-catching with her, she would have hesitated to wear it, so determined was she not to let him know she wanted to attract him. If only Miss Bateman had not told her of her matchmaking plans—and if only Giles had not guessed them either!

Reaching for the prettiest of her cotton dresses, she slipped it on. It had a softly flared skirt and a simple bodice whose narrow straps left her shoulders bare. She brushed her hair, burnished by the Indian sun and more gold than honey, so that it swung round her head like a silken swathe. It was, she decided critically, one of the most attractive things about her. With buoyant steps she left her bedroom and went downstairs.

Entering the bar she saw Giles before he saw her, and her heart turned over at the sight of him. Even a woman seeing him for the first time could not fail to be impressed by everything about him; his tall upright carriage, his perfectly delineated features and his amazing gold eyes which were now roving the room. They came to rest on her, and at once he rose and came forward to lead her back to the table. Without asking what she wanted to drink, he presented her with a fruit concoction, then suggested she take it to the table in the dining-room.

'A big party of Japanese tourists will be descending in about five minutes and I'd like to get our order in before they arrive,' he explained.

It was a valid point and she followed him into the dining-room, which had the muted coloured carpeting, piped music and tubular-shaped furniture of a cafeteria. But the food was Indian and excellent, and Giles ordered for them both, and then insisted she devote herself to eating and not making conversation. Abby was surprisingly glad to obey him. She was tired after her afternoon's exertions and was happy to be near him; to savour his looks and to store up every detail about him, so that in the winter of her life she could, like a squirrel, subsist.

They had reached the coffee stage and Giles was pouring himself a second cup when she saw his whole body stiffen. Turning slightly, she followed his startled gaze and saw Vicky Laughton and her husband walking into the dining-room. The couple saw them immediately and at once came over to the table.

'I'd no idea you were down here,' said Anthony Laughton. 'Vicky and I only decided to come on the spur of the moment—at least it was Vicky's idea, and being an obedient husband, I obeyed her!'

'And so you should,' Vicky smiled. 'After you left me alone in Bombay while you went off looking for birds.'

'*At* birds,' her husband chuckled. 'And they were feathered ones.'

'It might make you more exciting if it were the other kind,' came the drawling reply, and Abby knew she did not imagine the look of hurt that was momentarily visible in Anthony Laughton's pale eyes.

'Isn't Aunt Mattie here?' Vicky spoke directly to Giles. 'Or have we interrupted something special?'

Abby's cheeks burned, but Giles appeared indifferent. 'My aunt's having dinner in her room. If I wanted to take Abby away for a private jaunt I'd make sure it was too private for anyone to know.'

Vicky gave a shrill of laughter. 'How stuffy you've become! Living in India hasn't improved you.'

'We can't all have the same morals,' her husband interposed.

'Giles and I always agreed on that point.' Vicky's eyes were still glittering brightly, and the look she flashed Abby held no friendliness. 'You're certainly seeing a lot of India, Miss West.'

'No more than most tourists,' Abby replied. 'There's a circuit we all seem to follow.'

'Not my wife,' said Anthony Laughton. 'She makes her own itinerary. Coming here wasn't part of it.'

'You'll be glad you came once you've seen the caves,' said his wife, and looked at Giles again. 'How about joining forces with us tomorrow?'

'We've already been to Ellora,' Giles said. 'Tomorrow we're going to Ajanta.'

'Then we'll try to revise our plans and join you. Shall we meet in the bar after dinner?'

'Why not?' Giles replied, and half rose as Vicky followed her husband to a table some distance away.

Abby looked at Giles, waiting for him to make some comment on Vicky's arrival here, but he continued with his meal in silence, so that Abby was forced to speak first.

'Did you know they were coming here?' she asked.

'Is that a question or an accusation?' Giles put down

his fork sharply on the plate. 'I told you once before that I dislike being judged.'

'I wasn't passing judgment!'

'Weren't you?'

She flushed. 'It ... I merely thought ...'

'I know exactly what you were thinking. And may I remind you that my ex-fiancée is with her husband. Or have you overlooked that little fact?'

Abby's lips trembled. She was unprepared for his eruption of temper, though she knew she had only herself to blame for it. His mouth was thin with anger and his eyes smouldered like yellow coals as he pushed back his chair and stood up. Hurriedly she followed suit.

'I'll go to my room if you don't mind,' she said as they reached the entrance of the cocktail lounge. 'You can wait here alone for your *friends*.'

'Oh no, you don't.' Firmly he pulled her into the bar beside him.

Knowing he expected her to try to pull away, she relaxed and sedately seated herself beside him on a settee, hiding her triumph as she saw him give her a puzzled look.

'I can't make you out,' he said, half to himself. 'I know we got off on the wrong foot—for which I blame myself—and I can understand if you still see me as a curmudgeon. But I've given you no reason to see me as the world's worst rake!'

'I don't see you that way at all. We just have different standards and I'm not saying that mine are more acceptable than yours.'

'But you think they are, don't you?'

'One always thinks one's own morality is the best.'

'Have you never been in love with the wrong man?'

he countered. 'Or are you one of those lucky people who only fall in love to order?'

'I've never been in love,' she said firmly. 'And from what I've seen of people who are, I hope it never happens to me.'

'Keep behaving the way you do, and it won't.'

Her mouth quivered, but she refused to let him see how hurt she was.

'You're not only innocent and naïve,' he went on, 'but also rigid and narrow-minded. I don't think you're a fruit that will ripen after all. I've an idea you've already withered on the bough.'

With a gasp she jumped up. This was more than she could take, and no amount of will-power could hide the tears that shimmered in her eyes. 'I'm going to bed,' she choked, 'and please don't try and stop me!'

Once in her room Abby flung herself on the bed in a storm of weeping, and she was physically exhausted before it finally subsided and she sat up at last and wiped her eyes.

'You're nothing but a Little Miss Nobody,' she said to herself in the dressing-table mirror. 'Why should it surprise you that Giles sees you that way? And what right do you have to make any comments about his behaviour? It's not your business if he wants to go to bed with a hundred Vicky Laughtons!' After which ridiculous comment she undressed and went to sit by the window, hoping the tranquillity of the night would soothe her.

But Vicky's face seemed visible in the glass: sly, provocative, beautiful. There had been a look on it that had convinced Abby she had come to Aurangabad deliberately to be with Giles. And Anthony Laughton knew it too. Yet if he suspected his wife's feelings for the man she had once been going to marry, why had he left her alone in Bombay, knowing Giles was there? Had he done it deliberately in order to give her a chance to make up her mind what she wanted to do with her future? Yet it was not Vicky alone who could decide that future, Giles too had to make his decision.

Dispiritedly Abby climbed into bed and switched off the light. Darkness flooded over her, but it was no darker than her mood, and she lay for a long time before she slowly sank into sleep.

CHAPTER TWELVE

ONLY the knowledge that Miss Bateman would be distressed if she did not go on the trip to Ajanta next day prevented Abby from pleading illness and staying behind. She did genuinely have a headache, but knew that to use it as an excuse was insufficient and, fortifying herself with aspirins and strong tea, left her room.

The face she presented to the world was her usual calm one, though it elicited a disagreeable scowl from Giles, who was already at breakfast with his aunt. He looked tired and depressed, though whether this was because the presence of his lady love had made him sleep badly, or because he had a guilty conscience, she did not know.

Nor do I care, she told herself firmly. Giles Farrow can do what he likes with his life. If he hasn't the sense to realise he'll mess it up all over again if he lets Vicky Laughton come back into it, then he deserves to have her!

Miss Bateman was the only member of their trio who looked her usual confident, unflappable self as they left the hotel. In flat-heeled shoes and disreputable sun-hat, she was the epitome of the intrepid British sight-seer. Abby felt tiny walking beside her, and positively minuscule alongside Giles, who topped her by a head and shoulders. He made no attempt at conversation and silently waited for them to get into the back of the car before taking his usual position next to the driver.

'We have a long journey ahead of us, Abby,' Miss

Bateman said. 'Sixty uncomfortable miles.'

The statement proved to be no exaggeration. Apart from the poor condition of the road, they were constantly hampered by pedestrians, who jaywalked in front of them and deliberately slowed them down in order to peer into the car and grin at them in the most friendly fashion. They drove through many villages, some no more than a huddle of mud huts, others larger, with the ubiquitous single-storey shops and burning braziers from which one could obtain—if undeterred by the question of hygiene—all sorts of titbits.

Abby wondered what would happen to these villages when the dry, dusty earth became a sea of churning mud during the rainy season, and with a shudder she turned away from the open sewage. Almost immediately she felt guilty for closing her eyes to the degradation around her, knowing it was important for her not to forget or ignore the fact that so many of the people in this vast continent subsisted below the starvation level.

Two hours' hard driving through scrubland and cotton fields finally brought them to Ajanta. It was a crescent-shaped ravine, in which some twenty-nine caves had been carved. They had first been discovered in 1819, when a group of British officers on a tiger-hunt had tried to catch an escaping wounded animal who had suddenly seemed to disappear into the very heart of the mountainside. One of the officers, Captain John Smith, had gone in pursuit and, climbing halfway up the mountain, had discovered rough steps carved into its rocky side. Carefully hacking away the foliage to give himself a better footing, he had seen that the steps led to the entrance of a cave, its entrance so heavily blocked by undergrowth that had he not been within a few

inches of it he would never have discovered its
existence.

Further exploration disclosed a whole series of
caves: Buddhist shrines constructed more than two
thousand years before. Unlike those of Ellora, these
were tunnelled into the heart of the mountain, and their
rocky walls were ground smooth and covered with
elaborate, highly-coloured and sophisticated paintings.
Unfortunately, exposure to the air, without sufficient
protection, had caused many of them to crumble and
disappear before the Indian Department of Archaeology came to the rescue. But those that were left were a
unique example of ancient art, and showed a three-
dimensional quality that had not been found in any
painting of similar age anywhere else in the world.

As Abby's tour of the caves began, it soon became
clear that Giles had been here many times. He knew the
best caves to see, as well as the history of each painting
depicted, and explained them concisely yet lucidly.
Abby felt as if she were looking at Persian prints
enormously magnified, for many of the paintings had
the same vivid colours and plethora of detail. But unlike
Persian art, where people were all given blank expres-
sions, these showed various emotions.

Walking from cave to cave was tiring, for not only
were there a great many steps to climb, but there were
also people, so many that they were sometimes forced
to wait outside a cave until a group of tourists had left
and they themselves were allowed in. By noon Miss
Bateman admitted herself beaten, and announced she
was going to have a rest.

'But don't let that stop you two from exploring. I'll
sit in the shade and wait for you.'

'We can all do with a rest,' said Giles, and promptly

perched on the edge of the wall which had been built along the outside of the steps, a necessary protection to prevent people falling down the ravine.

Abby joined him by the wall, but was careful to keep her distance from him as she peered over the edge. Far below, the heavy undergrowth had been hacked away and a small garden cleared, and here she could make out Indian children lolling on the ground as they waited for tourists to come their way, when they would immediately resume their begging.

With a sigh, she sat on one of the steps and stared at the cave in front of her. Its entrance was protected by a wooden door, which was locked at night to prevent vandals destroying the paintings and statues. Alongside the door small niches had been dug out in the rock, each one barely big enough to hold a man. In these, thousands of years ago, Buddhist monks had kneeled in prayer, some of them remaining in the same position for days at a time. It was a religious devotion to which she herself could never have aspired: even the thought of it was so emotionally claustrophobic that she quickly averted her gaze and stared at the winding path, thick with slowly moving sightseers. There were not many foreign tourists, but Indian ones too, which surprised her until she remembered that for many of them, coming here was a religious experience. Ahead of her, among the sea of dark heads, she saw one that had a burnished glint, and with a sense of shock she recognised Vicky Laughton; so the girl had persuaded her husband to come to Ajanta after all! Next to her, Abby heard Giles' sharp indrawn breath, and knew that he too had seen the woman.

'Vicky and her husband are here,' he said casually to his aunt. 'She arrived in Aurangabad last night.'

'That doesn't surprise me,' Miss Bateman snorted. 'Considering she flew six thousand miles to see you again, a little journey from Bombay wouldn't deter her.'

'I'm beginning to see where Abby gets her bias,' he said so dryly that his aunt looked at Abby in surprise.

'Have you been trying to make Giles see reason too?'

Abby coloured. Having the question put to her so bluntly made her see how impertinent she had been to proffer her opinion to a man she barely knew. No wonder he had been angry!

'So we meet again!'

Vicky's light voice carried across the warm air as she came gracefully down the steps and stopped in front of them. In pale silk dress and matching low-heeled shoes, she looked unaffected by the exertion or the heat, though her husband was red-faced and puffing, which made him look every one of his twenty senior years. No wonder Vicky preferred Giles!

Abby looked out across the ravine and pretended to concentrate on the view, but she was painfully aware of the rise and fall of Vicky's voice and the deep tones of Giles' laugh. She wished she were a million miles away, and was so intent on this that she jumped visibly when Giles spoke to her.

'I think we should start moving again, Abby.'

She stood up, conscious of Vicky's scarlet-tipped hand resting on his arm.

'I'm sure Miss West would prefer to go with Aunt Mattie,' said Vicky. 'I know Tony will. He hates walking fast.'

'I've no intention of walking fast,' Giles stated. 'And it's much better if we all stick together. But if you and your husband want to go at your own pace ...'

'Of course not,' Vicky smiled. 'I'm sure you'll be a much better guide than Tony.'

Keeping a firm grip on his arm, she moved ahead with him, and Abby, seeing the scowl on Miss Bateman's face, knew her employer was angry at the way in which her nephew had allowed himself to be commandeered. But what was the point of anyone trying to come between Giles and his ex-fiancée? If Vicky had made up her mind to leave her husband and return to him, he alone was the sole arbiter of whether or not she succeeded. And from the way he was behaving, it was hard to doubt that she would.

Involuntarily Abby looked at Anthony Laughton. He was walking beside her but watching his wife with the look of a hurt dog. Abby wanted to shake him. Didn't he know that the only way to hold someone of his wife's temperament was to be forceful and vigorous, and that to look so vulnerable would only be interpreted as weakness?

'It seems you're stuck with me, Miss West,' he said, as Giles and Vicky were soon some ten yards ahead of them.

'I'm sure you're every bit as knowledgeable as Giles,' Abby smiled, noticing the heavy guidebook he was carrying.

'What I lack in knowledge, I make up for in enthusiasm!' At her chuckle he brightened. 'Would you like me to tell you about each cave as we go along?'

She nodded, seeing this as one way of precluding any other kind of conversation, but was soon so genuinely interested in what he was telling her that she lost all self-consciousness with him. For the most part, the interiors of the caves were only faintly illumined, though usually one, and sometimes two walls were lit by arc lamps to show the paintings in fullest detail. Even so, it was not always easy to see them, so thick were the throngs of people around them.

'This next cave has a remarkable statue of Buddha,' Anthony Laughton told her, and guided her past milling tourists to the back of a vast cave where, in a small inner sanctum, was a large carved statue of Buddha, sitting cross-legged on a lotus flower.

'What's different about this one?' she asked. 'I've seen hundreds like it.'

'But not with quite such a serene face. Concentrate on it, Miss West, and you'll know what I mean.'

Abby did so, then moved closer to it. Her companion had stepped away and she was alone in the alcove. She looked up into the face of the statue, then moved a couple of steps round its side in order to look at the profile. From the corner of her eye she saw a blur of pale material and slender arms uplifted around a dark form. For an instant she hesitated, then swiftly drew back. But the picture of Vicky Laughton in Giles' arms was etched on her brain like ink on a printing block.

Unable to bear any proximity with them, she stumbled into the main part of the cave and moved blindly between the jostling people until, more by luck than judgment, she found herself standing beside Anthony Laughton and Miss Bateman.

'Have you seen anything of Giles?' her employer asked.

Unable to speak, Abby shook her head, then turned and pretended to look at one of the colourful scenes depicted on the cave wall above her head. Again she heard Miss Bateman speak and knew that Giles and Vicky had rejoined them.

'Why did you disappear and leave us?' he asked his aunt. 'I told you we should stick together.'

'In this crowd?' the old lady scoffed. 'The only sticking I'm likely to do is to my clothes!'

'Then I suggest we call it a day,' he said at once. 'You've done more than enough.'

'I agree,' came the rueful reply. 'You go ahead with Abby and I'll return to the car.'

'Why don't you all come back in *our* car?' Vicky suggested. 'We managed to get an air-conditioned one.'

The prospect of sitting in close confines with Giles and the woman he loved made Abby search for an excuse to refuse.

'I'd like to stay behind and talk to some of the artists who are working here,' she said, and pointed to a large wooden easel that was perched on a scaffolding. There was a half-finished painting on it, though the artist was nowhere to be seen.

'I doubt if he'll come back while the tourists are still here,' Giles informed her. 'They mostly work early in the morning and never do more than four hours at a stretch, because of the strain on their eyes. But if you're interested in seeing them work I can arrange it for you tomorrow.'

'I'd still like to stay on now,' Abby persisted. 'I can always get a lift back with someone from the hotel.'

Everyone moved towards the exit, except Giles, who lagged behind.

'What's wrong, Abby? You're annoyed about something.'

'No, I'm not.'

'You are.' His eyes glinted with anger. 'I suppose you think I arranged to meet Vicky here?'

'I've given up thinking about you and Mrs Laughton. What you do is your own business.'

'One day I'll shake you so hard,' he said with quiet vehemence, though anyone watching him, as Vicky was doing from the entrance, would have supposed him to be making a casual comment.

Abby watched him go and wished she was going with him. But it was too late to change her mind, and she continued her exploration, moving slowly from one cave to another.

Gradually the intricate beauty of what she was seeing began to calm her perturbed mind, making her realise how futile her problems would be a hundred years from now, as were the problems of these men who had laboured so hard to create this world among the rocks. Yet the men who had worked and died here had been Buddhist priests, loving only their religion and turning away from women; not for them the jumbled emotions of love and hate, ecstasy and pain.

Deeply depressed by the thought of her loveless future, she leaned against one of the niches carved into the wall. Perhaps lunch would revive her spirits. It was only then that she remembered her luncheon pack, left in the car and now speeding on its way back to Aurangabad. That meant she would have to go all the way down to the bottom of the ravine and the cafeteria that had been built there.

Yet she was too tired to face the climb, and she perched inside the niche to relax for a short while. The stone wall was cool against her skin and she folded her cardigan into a pillow and leaned upon it. She would close her eyes; it would help her energy to return more quickly.

A severe cramp in her legs brought Abby back to consciousness. Startled by the darkness, she did not know where she was, and it was only when she sat up straight and felt a hard knob of rock dig into her shoulder that she realised she was inside one of the small stone niches.

With a gasp of fright she rose. There was no one in the cave. She must have been sleeping for hours. She looked at her watch, glad that the hands were luminous, and saw it was seven o'clock. No wonder she was alone! She looked around her again, and knew it was true. There was not a soul to be seen, nor a light to be glimpsed. She was alone in a cave, high up in a mountain, without anyone around her except the ghosts of the past.

Her heart was beating fast and she drew several deep breaths and warned herself not to panic. Though the place was as quiet as the grave, it was not a grave; though it appeared to be in the wilds of the jungle, it was only a matter of miles from the nearest village. But she gained no comfort from these thoughts and told herself firmly that only a short while ago there had been hundreds of sightseers here and that there would be hundreds more tomorrow. But tomorrow was a long way off, and there was still tonight to live through.

She put on her cardigan, for the air had grown cool, and she knew that before long it would be colder still. Gingerly picking her way in the gloom, she reached the entrance. The door was closed and for one heart-stopping moment, as she turned the handle, she was afraid it was locked and she would not be able to get out. But the door did move, albeit creakily, and she found herself outside in the blessed fresh air. Gulping happily, she began to make her way down the long flight of rocky steps.

She knew that in the dusk it would take her more than an hour to reach the entrance, and she plodded on. Twice she lost her way, once ending up in a cul-de-sac and the other against a heavy wood door that looked if it were the entrance to a cave that had not yet been fully reopened.

What an idiot she had been to fall asleep! Was it because she subconsciously wanted to block out the present and take refuge in dreamless slumber, where Giles did not exist?

Irritably telling herself not to waste time asking questions she could not answer, she negotiated a perilously steep flight of steps. The thin crescent moon was covered by a layer of cloud and, as the darkness intensified, an animal screeched somewhere in the distance. Nervously she wondered what sort of creature could be wandering on a mountainside at night. The officers who had first discovered these caves had been tiger-hunting. Yet there were no tigers in India now—or were there?

Something slithered past her in the blackness and she stiffened and peered through the foliage that bordered the steps. But there was nothing to be seen, and she was not sure if she had imagined it. Her nerves still jangling, she quickened her pace.

She was halfway down when the accident happened.

Grown careless by the ease with which she was managing to descend, she grew careless and did not grasp the side of the wall firmly. Her foot slipped on some wet vegetation and she tumbled down three steep steps. Her legs buckled beneath her and she sprawled flat on the rough ground.

For several breathless moments she lay there, then muttering at her own stupidity she got up. At least, she attempted to do so, but the instant she put her weight on her left foot, the darkness around her became streaked with red as fiery pain shot through her ankle. With another cry she sank to her knees, and it was several moments before the pain eased sufficiently for her to become aware of her surroundings again.

Gingerly she put her hand to her foot, wincing as her fingers touched the ankle bone. It did not seem to be broken. Tentatively she wriggled her toes. The pain was bad but bearable. Perhaps if she rested it for a short while it would ease sufficiently for her to hobble on it. She lowered her foot to the ground again. The moment she did so, the pain became excruciating, and she knew it would not be able to bear her weight.

A nice kettle of fish this was! Like it or not, it looked as if she was stuck here until the morning, when the caves were re-opened. A sudden thought occurred to her. These caves were run by the Department of Archaeology, and it was logical to assume they had a night-watchman on duty. Lifting her head, she began to shout. Her voice did not seem to penetrate far and she knew that unless the watchman were close at hand, he would never hear her. Her only hope was to push on, however slow her progress.

Careful not to jerk her ankle, she slid from one step down to the next. Although it would take her hours to make any progress, it was better than sitting still.

An hour later found her only twenty yards further on. The slightest unwary movement sent such a fierce jab through her foot that on two occasions she nearly fainted, and now she was almost frightened to move at all.

Even when she reached the entrance she would still have the steep climb down the rest of the mountainside to the bottom of the ravine. It was here that coaches were parked during the day, and where some fifty stalls were erected each morning and set out with mounds of beads and bangles. But where did the stallkeepers go at night? At best the only transport they might have would be a bicycle, and some of them were too poor even to have that. Remembering how the beggars slept in Bombay, she decided there was a distinct possibility that some of the stallkeepers made their homes on the bare earth at the back of their stall.

Encouraged by this thought, she inched forward again, only stopping as she remembered the Indian who had pestered her this morning as she had left the car, and whom Giles had briskly shoved aside. There had been something in the Indian's eyes that had frightened her, and suddenly her intention of seeking help resolved itself into a determination to stay hidden in one of the alcoves until daylight brought the guides and tourists.

Scrambling across the steps to the niche cut beside the door of the cave nearest to her, she crawled inside. Gradually her trembling ceased. In this same alcove, two thousand years ago, a Buddhist monk had lived, praying in the temple during the day and sleeping in this niche at night. The thought of him gave her comfort, and she relaxed.

Time passed slowly. Her limbs were numb. It was becoming increasingly difficult to keep up her spirits and she silently recited all the poems she could remember. One of them remained with her more vividly than the rest, and she repeated it to herself continually.

> 'We are the music makers,
> And we are the dreamers of dreams,
> Wandering by lone sea-breakers,
> And sitting by desolate streams.'

That's me, Abby thought dismally. A dreamer of dreams that will never come true.

An image of Giles flashed before her eyes and she lowered her head upon her hands and wept.

Something suddenly alerted her, and she stiffened

and sat up, not sure whether she had imagined it. But no, the sound came again and she heard her name called.

In disbelieving wonder, she answered. 'I'm here, I'm here!'

'Keep calling!' the voice cried, and though it was faint, she recognised it to be Giles'.

In front of her a light flashed, then disappeared as the path curved. When she saw it again it was nearer and brighter. Obeying Giles' order, she called intermittently until all at once he was kneeling beside her and gripping her by the shoulders.

'What the hell happened to you?' There was no solicitude in his voice, only raw anger. 'Are you out of your mind, sitting here like this? You should at least have had the sense to keep moving in this cold temperature!'

'I can't move,' she croaked. 'I'm hurt.'

His grip became fiercer. 'How hurt?'

'N-not badly.' Reaction was beginning to affect her and she was hard put to it not to burst into tears. 'I—I twisted my ankle. I fell off a s-step and ...'

Muttering an imprecation, Giles lifted her gently into his arms.

'It's a waste of time for me to look at it here. Put your arm round my neck and hold the torch with the other. That'll be the safest way of getting us both down to ground level without having another accident.'

She obeyed him, gritting her teeth as the motion sent sharp stabs of pain through her ankle. Feeling her tension, he did not speak, and it was only when they reached the end of the steps and he was walking on the relatively flat path that he did so.

'How come you got left behind?' he asked.

'I sat down to have a rest. I only meant to close my eyes for a minute, but——'

'You bloody little fool!'

His attack was so unexpected that the self-pity which had been threatening to engulf her disappeared completely.

'How dare you say that! Do you think I *wanted* to be locked in? That I *wanted* to fall and put myself through this misery? You're a swine, Giles Farrow, a heartless, uncaring swine!'

'I care enough to have spent the last four hours traipsing the road from the hotel to back here. I thought someone might have given you a lift and you'd quarrelled with them.'

'Quarrelled?' she questioned, not sure what he meant.

'That someone had made a pass at you and you'd run away from them.'

She tried to imagine herself escaping from a car with a lecherous, perspiring male racing after her, and the picture was so amusing that she began to laugh.

'What's so funny?' Giles growled.

She tried to answer him, but couldn't; her laughter was too intense, and quickly exploded into hysteria.

'Stop that!' Giles ordered, and shook her.

The movement sent a stab of pain through her foot and she gave a sharp cry. He gripped her more tightly against his chest and lowered his head until his cheek rested on her hair.

'Forgive me, Abby, I didn't mean to hurt you. But if you knew how worried we'd been ... The way I kept imagining you lying hurt somewhere ...'

She nestled closer to him and burrowed her face into the side of his neck. She was dimly aware of them reaching the bottom of the ravine and of being carefully placed in the back of a car and wrapped with blankets. Her shivering stopped and was replaced by the deep languor of exhaustion. She felt the car move beneath her but was too tired to open her eyes, and she only did so when she felt Giles' hands upon her shoulders again.

'We've arrived,' he said briefly and, not giving her a chance to move, lifted her bodily from the car.

As they went through the glass doors, she saw people milling around in the lobby and became aware of how dishevelled she must look, and how conspicuous being held in his arms.

'Please put me down,' she whispered. 'If I can hold on to you, I can manage to hobble.'

Ignoring her, he strode forward through the swing doors, and at once they were surrounded by curious faces and a babble of voices all asking questions. Giles pushed his way through the crowd towards the reception desk and asked for the key of her room.

'The doctor is already here, Mr Farrow,' the clerk said. 'Shall I send him up?'

'Yes.'

'How did you know I'd need a doctor?' Abby asked.

'I was afraid you might need an undertaker,' he replied, tight-lipped, and again she was aware of the anger in him. Still holding her, he turned from the desk and, as he did so, she saw Vicky Laughton and Miss Bateman coming towards them.

'My dear child!' Miss Bateman exclaimed in concern. 'Thank God you're alive! What happened to you?'

'I slipped and sprained my ankle. It was my own fault.'

'But why were you alone?'

'You'll have plenty of time to talk to Abby to-morrow,' said Giles. 'Right now she needs her ankle attended to, and a sedative.'

'Don't fuss so, Giles!'

Vicky's voice was as clear as a bell, but with a discordant tone to it that made Giles look at her keenly.

'All she did was to get lost,' Vicky continued. 'She wasn't in real danger.'

'Except from exposure,' he said evenly. 'And she could quite conceivably have fallen over the wall and killed herself.'

'But she didn't, so why make such a fuss?' Vicky's expression was spiteful as her eyes met Abby's. 'You'll be a seven days' wonder when you get back to Bombay. "Girl tourist lost among the shrines." If you can say you saw a couple of Buddhist ghosts roaming round them, you might even get yourself into the newspapers.'

Abby was so astonished at the attack that she did not know what to say. She had just decided that silence was probably the best defence, when Giles spoke. His voice was quiet, but because he was still holding her she felt the tension within him, and knew what an effort he was making not to let anyone see it.

'If Abby wanted to create interest in herself,' he said, 'all she needed to do was to stop keeping our engagement a secret.'

'Your what?' Vicky exclaimed.

'Our engagement. That would make her more than a seven days' wonder, don't you think?' He half lowered his head to Abby, a smile tilting his mouth. 'I've been telling you for days that it was silly for us to go on pretending, but you're such a shy little thing.'

'I knew it!' Miss Bateman interposed, beaming widely. 'I knew that the two of you were made for each other.'

'You should start writing romances instead of thrillers,' Vicky said scornfully, then swung back to Giles. 'I don't believe you. You're making it up.'

'Why should I?'

'Because you never said a word to me about it.'

'You'd be the last person I'd tell.' He shifted Abby's weight in his arms. 'Now, if you'll excuse me, I'd like to take Abby to her room.'

It was only when they were alone together in the lift that Abby found her tongue.

'I know you were angry with Mrs Laughton for what she said to me, but it was ridiculous of you to answer her the way you did. All you've done is to make me look a bigger fool.'

'We'll talk about it later.'

'We'll talk about it now,' she said crossly. 'Why did you have to pretend we're engaged?'

'I didn't like her attack on you,' he said, 'and I wanted to hurt her.'

'By using me—or doesn't it matter to you if you hurt me instead?'

'It wasn't my intention to hurt you,' he said swiftly, and before she could reply, the lift doors opened and she saw the doctor standing outside her room.

Abby had no further chance to talk alone with Giles, which was a good thing, she decided as she lay on the bed and allowed her ankle to be examined. In her present mood she might say things she would regret when she was more in control of herself.

'I'll leave you to get settled,' Giles said. 'I'll be downstairs if the doctor wants me—or if you do.'

'You're the last person I want,' she said bluntly. 'Please go away.'

The door closed behind her and the doctor gave her a surprised look.

'You are in pain,' he said, as if seeking a reason for what he considered such strange behaviour.

'Not my foot,' she replied, and wondered what he would say if she asked him if he had a medicament for a broken heart.

CHAPTER THIRTEEN

THE sedative which the doctor gave Abby prevented her from any further thought for the rest of what was left of the night, and when she awoke in the morning, her ankle strapped but the pain bearable, she was in a far more cohesive state of mind to try to work out the real reason why Giles had pretended they were engaged.

What seemed obvious to her was his fear of being trapped again by Vicky. He was afraid that if he were still seen to be free, he would be far more vulnerable. Well, she had wanted him to put up a fight against his ex-fiancée, but had never foreseen that he would use herself as the weapon.

There was a tap at the door, and thinking it was room service, she bade them enter. But it was Giles who came in, face still pale, but his usual impeccable self.

'You look better,' he said, and came to stand at the foot of the bed, one hand in the pocket of his white linen jacket. 'As soon as you've had breakfast I'm taking you to the hospital to have your ankle X-rayed.'

'There are no bones broken,' she replied. 'Please don't fuss.'

'You might have a slight fracture, and it's better to be safe than sorry.'

'That doesn't just apply to my ankle.'

He gave a long-drawn-out sigh. 'I suppose you're referring to what I said to Vicky.'

'Did you expect me not to refer to it?'

She sat further up in bed, then became aware of her flimsy nightdress, and pulled the sheet hastily up around her breasts.

'We can't go on with this engagement, Giles. If you won't tell Mrs Laughton it was a joke, then I will.'

'What makes you think it was a joke?'

'You could tell her the truth, if you prefer,' Abby replied, ignoring his question. 'And say that the only way you can stand up to her is to hide behind another woman's skirts! And don't bother denying it,' she said, as he made to speak, 'because I saw you both yesterday in one of the caves—and you were damned lucky her husband didn't see you, too.'

'So it *was* you,' Giles said quietly. 'Is that why you're so angry with me?'

'Even if I hadn't seen you kissing her, I would have been angry over this engagement. Do you think I don't know you want to use me as a cover?'

Her voice shook, but she managed to control it. Giles had gone to stand by the window and all she could see of him was his beautifully etched profile. She noticed the springiness of his hair and the nervous movement with which he ran his hand across the top of it, showing her that for all his calm manner he was as perturbed as she was. The knowledge softened her mood towards him, helping her to see how difficult it must be for a man of his temperament to know he could not stop wanting another man's wife. But why had he used her as an escape?

'Have I hurt you so deeply?' he asked into the silence. 'Do you find it so repugnant to be engaged to me?'

'I find it repugnant to be *used*!'

'But not to be engaged to me,' he said swiftly. 'You don't mind that?'

Afraid of giving herself away, she said evenly, 'Of course I mind the pretence. But I—but I can see that most girls would be flattered by it.'

He was back by the foot of her bed, his hands folded across his chest. 'But not you, I take it?'

'No, not me. I'm glad you're trying to fight your feelings for Mrs Laughton, but I—but I don't want to be the weapon you use.'

'So you'll break the engagement and send me to the wolves—or should I say vixen?'

She didn't smile. 'I'm sure you're clever enough to take care of yourself.'

'Not as clever as you imagine. In fact, when I think of it, exceptionally stupid.'

He moved to the side of the bed and she was conscious of how dishevelled she must look. Clutching the sheet with one hand, she smoothed her hair with the other.

'I do wish you'd go and leave me alone,' she said petulantly.

'You've no need to be embarrassed. If all women looked as lovely as you do when they first woke up, the beauty companies would be out of business.'

'Thanks,' she said, too irritable to be complimented. 'But you needn't think that flattery will get me to do as you want.'

'Nothing was further from my mind.'

She gave him a sharp look, but his expression was serious. With all her heart she wished their engagement was a real one, and that Giles might one day come to love her. But such thoughts were foolish. He was a man of the world and probably considered her naïve in the extreme.

'I suppose I seem very young to you,' she said jerkily. 'That's why you think you can use me when it suits you.'

'I wouldn't put it quite that way.'

His gaze moved from her face to the curve of her shoulders, and hurriedly she pulled the sheet higher.

'You know what I mean,' she protested. 'Don't deliberately misunderstand me.'

'But you don't know what I mean,' he replied. 'Why do you always denigrate yourself, Abby? You're young and innocent, I agree, but you have a quiet beauty that becomes considerably stronger the moment one starts to notice it.'

This time she could not control her temper. 'If you don't stop playing with me, Giles, I'll go down this minute and tell your lady friend you were lying to her last night!'

'You mean you weren't going to do that anyway?' he asked, in pretended surprise. Then seeing she was still struggling with her temper, he leaned forward and, wrapping the sheet more carefully about her, pulled her against him and gave her a brief hug.

'I knew I could rely on you,' he said huskily. 'Just carry on with the act for a little while. It means everything to me.'

Glad that he did not know it meant everything to her—though in a different way—Abby's sigh gave him the promise he needed, and reminding her that he would be back to carry her down to the car within the hour, he left her to wait for her breakfast.

The medical centre in Aurangabad was an imposing concrete structure, far more lavish in design than was required in such a small place. But then this was something Abby had noticed in many of the small towns she passed through during her trip.

'You're letting your prejudice show,' said Giles.

'How did you know what I was thinking?'

'You have an expressive face.'

'Then perhaps you'd care to comment on my thoughts?'

In the act of carrying her up the steps, Giles paused to look into her face.

'You find the Indian love of education somewhat exaggerated, and wish they would concentrate on quality rather than quantity.'

'Something like that,' she said cautiously. 'Though I can see that in a country of this size, quantity may be more necessary.'

'They have quality too; and in the field of astronomy and science they're excellent.'

'You like the Indians, don't you?'

'I like *people*,' he replied. 'I don't understand how man can think in terms of conquering space when he hasn't yet learned how to stop dividing earth up into segments.'

Abby agreed wholeheartedly with what Giles had said, and found it incredible that a man of his intelligence could be in love with someone as shallow as Vicky Laughton. Of course it was easy to understand why Vicky wanted *him*. The reason brought a blush to Abby's cheeks, and Giles noticed it.

'You look very pretty when you blush,' he said. 'Though you look equally pretty when you don't.'

'Still acting, Giles? There's no one here to see you.'

'Does a man have to be acting to pay you a compliment?'

'*You* would have to.'

'Why me?'

'Because I'm not your type.'

He looked rueful. 'You sound glad that you're not.'

'I am,' she said sharply. 'We've been brought together by circumstances, but in the ordinary course of events we would never have met.'

'But now we have, don't you think we should make the best of it? Or do I have to keep reminding you that we're supposed to be friends—as well as being temporarily engaged?'

'We can never be friends, and our engagement won't fool anyone who knows you. A man who loved Mrs Laughton couldn't fancy someone like me. Now stop standing here holding me,' she said irritably, 'and take me inside.'

Silently he obeyed her, and she was glad when a nurse met them at the door and they were no longer alone.

The X-ray showed there were no broken bones in Abby's ankle, though she was advised to rest it for at least a week, and Giles decided that since she was immobile, they might as well return to Bombay.

By dint of pulling some strings, he was able to obtain seats for them on the afternoon plane, and it was only when she hobbled down to the lobby, with the assistance of a maid, having flatly refused to call Giles for help, that she had her first encounter of the day with Vicky Laughton.

'What a surprise your engagement was,' said Vicky. 'I never knew you and Giles were such wonderful actors.'

'We wanted to keep it a secret,' Abby explained.

'How odd. Most engaged couples like to show each

other off; and all the girls I know would give their eye-teeth if they could announce that they were going to marry Giles.'

'I'm not most girls, Mrs Laughton. Perhaps that's why Giles loves me.'

The colour that stained the hollows beneath Vicky's cheekbones told Abby that her reply had hit home.

'I don't believe he loves you,' said Vicky. 'Giles feels guilty because he thinks he's breaking up my marriage. But as soon as he realises I'm going to leave Anthony anyway, he'll stop trying to fight me. We love each other and we have a right to our happiness.'

'What happened to your love when he asked you to marry him before?'

Vicky's blue eyes clouded with remorse. 'I couldn't face the prospect of travelling from one Indian village to another. I behaved like an idiot and I hurt both of us needlessly. I knew almost as soon as I'd married Anthony that I'd made a terrible mistake.'

'I'm not interested in your mistakes.' Abby longed to hit the coolly smiling face in front of her, but managed to control herself. 'The only person who could possibly care is Giles, and since he now loves *me* ...'

'If you believe that, you're a fool. The moment I'm free, Giles will come to me—even if you've succeeded in marrying him. Think of *that* when he's holding you in his arms and making love to you!'

Vicky spun round on her heels and walked quickly away, but Giles, stepping into the lobby, caught a glimpse of her.

'What was Vicky talking to you about?' he asked, coming over.

'You. She still intends to get a divorce and marry you.'

'I see.' He subjected her to an intense stare. 'It's obviously made you angry.'

'Only because it's shown me how pointless it is for us to go on with this engagement. Mrs Laughton knows it's a pretence.'

'Then marry me and show her she's wrong.'

Abby stared at him. The temptation to say yes was only momentary, yet enough to show her how easily love could make a fool of one's intelligence. What sort of happiness could she find married to a man who she knew was thinking of another woman each time he held her in his arms?

'Well, Abby?' Giles repeated. 'Why not do as I suggest and marry me?'

'Are you such a coward that the only way you can fight Mrs Laughton is to hide behind another woman's skirts?'

'You've said that to me before.' His tone was mild. 'But may I remind you I'd have a hard job hiding behind yours. Six foot two into five foot won't go!'

'You know what I mean.'

'Your bluntness leaves me in no doubt. You're so unwilling to help me that you'd happily send me to the lions.'

'Last night you said it was the wolves,' Abby retorted. 'And that's much more Mrs Laughton's genus. She's a vixen. If you haven't the strength to fight her on your own . . .'

'We can't all be as strong-minded as you,' he said, and scooping her up in his arms, carried her out to the waiting car.

At the airport he carried her too, ignoring her protests by saying he didn't have the patience to walk slowly beside her, which might have been a satisfactory reason but was not the one she had wanted to hear.

What a fool I am, she thought. Did I expect him to say he was holding me because he enjoyed it?

Making sure she was comfortably seated in the plane beside his aunt, Giles took a seat across the aisle and, immediately after take-off, was engrossed in a book. Abby watched him from the corner of her eye, disconcerted when he unexpectedly turned his head and their glances met. There was an odd glow in his eyes that she could not fathom, then it was gone, masked by his lids as he lowered his head to the page.

It was a relief to return to the house in Bombay, but Abby's hopes of spending a quiet week relaxing and resting her ankle came to naught, for she and Giles were inundated with invitations from his friends, who had heard of their engagement and were anxious to meet her.

'I can't imagine why you told anyone about me,' she said crossly one evening, when they were returning from a small dinner party given by an eminent Indian scientist in their honour. 'Don't you feel guilty at accepting hospitality under false pretences?'

'I do, now you've mentioned it,' he said. 'But there's another way of looking at it; we can only fool Vicky if we behave the way a normally engaged couple would.'

'You're certainly doing that,' Abby retorted, and thought of the solicitous way he had kept his arm around her waist as he had guided her to a chair in Professor Sundra's drawing-room, and the lover-like manner in which he had occasionally clasped her hand. They would all add to the storehouse of her memories of him, and she was afraid she would soon have so many memories to cherish that she would have no time for living and building a future for herself after they had parted.

'What a deep sigh you've given,' he commented as he

parked the car directly beside the front doorstep of the house. 'Is it such a strain for you to pretend you're a happily engaged young woman?'

'If you're my fiancé, it is,' she snapped.

'Poor Abby.' But there was no sympathy in his voice, only suppressed anger. 'And now, I'm afraid, I'm going to add to the strain.'

Before she could guess his intention, he swung her round in the seat and pulled her into his arms. He was a big man and, despite his thinness, whipcord-strong. She knew it was pointless to fight him and she forced herself to remain pliant, putting up no resistance to the pressure of his mouth on hers. Even when his ardour increased, she made herself unresponsive, though it cost her a great effort not to wind her arms around him and run her fingers over his thick hair and down the firm column of his neck. But she was not going to give him the satisfaction of responding. She would use every ounce of her will power never to give him that particular victory.

He lifted his mouth away from hers but still kept tight hold of her.

'Why are you pretending to be an iceberg, Abby?'

'It's not a pretence.'

'Yes, it is. You're too warmhearted not to have emotions.'

'Haven't you considered the possibility that *you* might not arouse them in me?'

There was a pause.

'No,' he said slowly, 'I hadn't. You're a normal young woman, and since I don't believe you find me physically repulsive, there must be another reason why you're so frigid with me.'

Petrified lest he discover what it was, she did the

only thing possible and went in to the attack, seeing this as her best form of defence.

'I don't find you repulsive, Giles, but that doesn't mean I find you attractive either. You're good-looking and occasionally amusing, and I know you have a high reputation in your profession. But it takes more than that to arouse my desire. If that makes me different from the other females you've known, then I'm sorry. But I'm not a doll to be picked up and cuddled when the mood takes you. So next time you feel the urge, I suggest you have a cold bath instead!'

Silently he got out of the car and came round the side, but before he could help her she had already scrambled out and was hobbling up the steps. In her effort to escape him she was too precipitate, and would have fallen had he not reached out and caught her. Still in silence, he lifted her up and carried her into the hall.

'I won't offer to take you to your bedroom in case my baser instincts get the better of me,' he said. 'So I'll leave you to manage the best way you can while I go and take a cold shower.'

She was halfway up the first flight—Giles having long since disappeared—when the bitter humour of the situation struck her, and she smiled. She had hurt Giles' vanity tonight, but it had been better than giving away her own feelings. It might also do him good to realise he couldn't always get what he wanted. As she thought of this, she remembered Vicky. She had resisted Giles too, and married someone else.

But now Vicky no longer wanted to resist him. Indeed, it was her singular lack of resistance that had frightened him into pretending he was going to marry someone else. As always when she thought of this, Abby was puzzled by his behaviour. He was not against divorce on religious grounds, so she could only assume he was fighting Vicky because he did not want the girl to think she could just crook her little finger and have him come running. Yet sooner or later he would run, and Abby hoped with all her heart that she would not be there to witness it.

Another week went by. The bandage was taken from her ankle, and she was fully mobile again with nothing to show for her mishap other than her continuing engagement to Giles. She had told Miss Bateman the truth about it, refusing to let that good lady believe her matchmaking hopes had succeeded.

'What a pity you and Giles are only pretending,' Miss Bateman said one afternoon towards the end of the second week, when they were sitting in the garden of the house awaiting the arrival of Mrs Chandris, in whose magnificent penthouse Abby had seen Giles re-encounter Vicky. 'Is there no hope of it becoming real?'

'No. Giles will eventually give in to Mrs Laughton. She's that sort of woman.'

'And what sort of woman are you, that you aren't willing to fight for him?'

Abby looked up quickly, but could not meet Miss Bateman's eyes and lie. Yet she was unwilling to tell the truth either, and instead she prevaricated.

'I'm doing all I can to help Giles, but in the end, the final resistance must come from him.'

'You haven't answered the question, my dear. You're in love with that nephew of mine and you should make an effort to get him.'

Abby forced a smile to her lips. 'Do you think people can be "got" so easily? Catching somebody's emotions isn't like fishing for tiddlers!'

'I'm not so sure—where men are concerned. They're very much like fish. Show them the right bait and they'll rise to it.'

It was all too easy for Abby to imagine Vicky Laughton as a piece of delectable bait, bobbing in the water ready to be snapped at by a hapless tiddler. Or didn't tiddlers go for bait? She frowned, annoyed by her fantasising, and relieved when Mrs Chandris was shown into the garden by a servant.

The next hour passed in idle gossip, and it was only when they were sipping weak Indian tea and chewing on some delectable sweetmeats that the conversation turned to Vicky Laughton.

'I understand her husband is returning to America and leaving her here. Apparently she's going to do a meditation course.'

'I can't see her meditating for long,' Miss Bateman stated. 'She isn't the type.'

'According to her husband she has become completely absorbed by the teachings of one of our gurus. And they do have amazing personalities, you know. They gather the most unlikely people as their disciples.'

'Maybe they do. But to become somebody's disciple you have to lose your own ego, and I can't see Vicky doing that for long.'

Mrs Chrandris gave a gentle smile. 'You should not discount the possibility of change for the better. That is why the human mind is unique. The contemplation of the soul can lead to greater knowledge and understanding of oneself.'

'The only soul Vicky will ever contemplate is a grilled one on a dish!' Miss Bateman replied.

Mrs Chandris laughed and changed the conversation, but after she had left, Abby returned to it and asked a question that had been in her mind for several days.

'What's going to happen to Giles when we go home? I know you were hoping to stay on until Mrs Laughton also left, but if she's going to take a meditation course here, she might be staying for months.'

'Then so will we,' Miss Bateman answered. 'Giles is happy to have us here, and one of the joys of being a writer is that I can continue with my work anywhere. Did I tell you I once wrote a book while I was hiking in the Appalachians? I was much younger then, of course, but——'

'Stop flannelling,' Abby interrupted.

'Flannelling?'

'You know what I mean. When are we going to leave India? I don't want to continue with my engagement. I've been happy to help Giles, but I—but I can't go on any longer.'

'If Vicky succeeds in trapping him,' said Miss Bateman gently, 'she will make him very unhappy.'

'I don't see why you should say that. He loves her and——'

'I don't believe he does.'

Abby wanted to believe this too, but knew it was foolish to let wishes try to disguise themselves as facts.

'He does love her, Miss Bateman. If he didn't, he wouldn't need to use me as his defence. And I'm tired of it. I want to leave India. If you want to stay on, then I'll make my own arrangements.'

'Even if it means you will no longer work for me?'

'I'm afraid so.' Abby was saddened by the knowledge, but could see no way out; much as she wished to stay with Miss Bateman, it was imperative for her own peace of mind that she stop seeing Giles.

'Very well, Abby,' sighed Miss Bateman. 'Telephone the airline and see if they can get us a flight out on Monday. You don't object to staying four days more, I hope?'

Abby shook her head and went into the house to make the arrangements before Giles returned home.

Since he had announced their engagement, he always dined with them, and even when he had papers to work on would bring them into the sitting-room rather than go into his study, which he had previously done. It was as if he wanted to carry on with the pretence of their engagement even when there was no one there to see it, and though she knew Miss Bateman interpreted it as a sign of his growing attraction for the girl who falsely wore his engagement ring, Abby saw it as a weakness; as a fear that if he were left alone he would brood upon Vicky and weaken his resolve.

When she returned to the garden, their flight booked, she looked around her with nostalgia. She had spent many happy hours here, particularly in the last two weeks, when Giles had frequently returned home for lunch and swum with her in the pool. Splashing about with him in the water, she had been able to forget that he was in love with someone else, and because the forgetting had become too frequent of late, she had seen the dangers and known she could only avoid them by running away.

'I must do some last-minute shopping,' Miss Bateman announced. 'What about you?'

'My suitcase is already bulging. So please don't ask me to go with you or I won't be able to resist temptation.'

Abby thought of this as she showered and changed for dinner later that evening. She was certainly resisting temptation by running away from Giles. She sat down at the dressing-table and stared at herself in the mirror. Unrequited love must be good for her, for she had never looked more blooming. Almost pretty, she thought, and then smiled as she knew how angry Giles would be at her deprecation of herself.

'I'm not so bad,' she mused aloud, and tightened the strap of her bra. The soft curves of her breasts were seen through the lacy material, which matched her brief panties. She had gained a little weight and it suited her, lessening the childishness of her curves and giving them a rounder, more voluptuous quality.

There was a sharp knock on the door and before she could say 'Come in,' Giles strode through and slammed it shut behind him. Startled, she half rose to reach for her dressing-gown, but he was standing in front of her, so embarrassingly close that she knew it would be safer to remain seated.

'How dare you make arrangements to go back to England?' he asked furiously. 'Don't you know I still want you here?'

Abby's swift reply was forestalled by the pallor of his face. She had never seen Giles in such a rage. His mouth was a thin line and his eyes were yellow as a tiger's and twice as menacing. She swallowed and tried to speak as reasonably as she could.

'I can't stay here for ever. You knew we'd be going back soon.'

'Not so soon. Tell me why.'

'Isn't the question obvious? I'm tired of pretending and listening to your friends prattle a load of nonsense about our future.'

'What nonsense?' he asked.

'About marriage and babies and that sort of rubbish.'

Afraid she might start to cry, and intent on putting as much distance between them as possible, she rummaged wildly in a drawer of the dressing-table for a slip. She found a wisp of peach silk and quickly put it on. As it slithered over her body she gained a little courage from its covering, and stood up to move away from him. But he refused to budge, and short of pushing past him, she had to remain where she was.

'I'm sorry you don't like talk of marriage and babies,' he bit out. 'I thought you were the type to want both.'

'I am. But not in these circumstances.'

'What's wrong with the circumstances? Marry me, Abby, and let's stop making it a pretence.'

'No.'

'Why not? You aren't in love with anyone else.'

'That doesn't mean I want to marry *you*.' She tried to sidle past him but again he blocked her way. 'Giles, please. Leave the room and let me finish dressing.'

'I'd rather you remain undressed,' he said huskily, and gripped her shoulders. 'I can't let you go, Abby. I won't!'

Abandoning all pretence of retaining her temper, Abby went to push him away. Her resistance was all he needed to set fire to his own temper, and he caught her hands and pushed them roughly down to her side. She tried to kick him and managed a sharp blow on his shins before he swung her off her feet and carried her over to the bed. He dumped her down on it and before she could lever herself up he flung himself across her. Her heart leapt and then began to race. But it was not with fright; only treacherous desire.

'Let me go, Giles,' she said, marvelling how calmly she managed to sound.

'Not yet,' he said thickly. 'I want to talk to you.'

'Then talk to me sitting up.'

'You'll run away.'

She did not deny it. 'I hate you!' she cried.

'I've given you no reason. I've been an exemplary fiancé.'

'The phoney lover,' she mocked.

'Neither a lover, nor phoney,' he said with un-expected savagery, and claimed violent possession of her mouth.

Ignited by his touch, her body automatically arched itself against his. The flimsy silk she wore was no barrier between them, and she heard the pounding of his heart and felt the tension of his muscles as he pressed her deeper into the softness of the bed.

'I won't let you go,' he muttered, and twined his fingers around the honey-gold strands of hair that splayed out on the pillow. Cupping her face with one hand, he made it impossible for her to turn her head, and stared intently into her eyes. 'You've taunted me and haunted me ever since I set eyes on you, and now you're going to take the consequences.'

'No!' She tried to struggle from under him, but he remained a heavy weight upon her. 'Please, Giles, let me go! You'll be sorry if you don't.'

'I'll be sorry if I do. Perhaps I should have taken you weeks ago. I've tried reason and flattery, and I've even tried jealousy, but nothing seems to work. So perhaps it's time for me to use force.'

'You're mad!' she gasped, and managed to get her hands free and push them against his chest. 'Let me go!'

'Never. You're mine.' His breath was warm on her skin as his head lowered again.

This time his lips did not seek hers but came to rest

on the shadow between her breasts, then moved along their curve leaving feather-light kisses all the way. The touch of them inflamed her, and though she tried to resist it, it was a losing battle. How could one fight something one wanted so much? It was as futile as Giles fighting his love for Vicky. The thought of Vicky was almost enough to bring Abby to her senses; almost, but not quite. With a soft moan she stopped fighting and gave herself up to the pleasure of his nearness, refusing to believe she would regret it when sanity returned.

Feeling her surrender, Giles loosened his grip on her, but only in order to gather her more closely to his body. But instead of kissing her again, he rested his cheek upon hers.

'I love you, Abby. How could you not have known?'

She was filled with momentary elation, then it disappeared. 'You don't need to lie to me, Giles, it isn't necessary.'

'Why should I lie? Do you think I'm putting on an act so that you'll let me go on making love to you? Is that the sort of swine you think I am?'

'Don't be harsh on yourself,' she whispered, stroking his hair and enjoying the vibrant feel of it beneath her hand. 'You've been hurt and you need love.'

'I've certainly been hurt,' he said, and to her utter astonishment began to laugh. 'Oh, Abby, you fool! You still don't know that you're the one who's hurting me. Vicky hasn't had the power to do that almost from the moment she left me.'

'But your aunt——'

'Aunt Matty's a writer and given to exaggeration,' he interrupted. 'Vicky hurt me badly in the beginning, but I soon realised she'd only wounded my pride and that the woman I thought she was didn't exist.'

'And am I the woman you thought Vicky was?' Abby asked dryly, knowing that if Giles said yes she would not believe him. But to her delight he shook his head violently, and his loud 'No!' was an explosion of sound in the room. 'You're nothing like I imagined Vicky to be. You're the exact opposite of the woman I dreamed of finding!'

He sat up on the bed and pulled her up with him, keeping his arm round her, so that she was leaning against his shoulder. 'You're not my ideal woman at all,' he continued with amusement. 'I always wanted someone tall and dark, who'd be docile by day and fiery at night!'

'And me?'

'You're fiery all the time!'

She giggled, still unable to believe he meant all he was saying. As if he was aware of this, Giles tilted up her face and looked intently into her eyes.

'I didn't love you when we first met. You irritated me and I was wary of the way you'd befriended my aunt. I couldn't believe anyone could be so genuinely caring about someone they hardly knew. But pretty soon I realised you were exactly the way you seemed; that you thought of others before you thought of yourself. From then on I was lost.'

'You hid your feelings well,' she said ruefully. 'That night at the Chandrises' party when you saw Vicky, you looked absolutely shattered.'

'I was. But not because I loved her. It was a shock, nothing more.'

'Why did you have lunch with her the following day?'

'Because she telephoned me and asked me. I was

curious to know what was in her mind. In fact,' he added slowly, 'I had a pretty good idea.'

'And kissing her in the cave the other day? Was that at her invitation too?'

'At the risk of sounding ungallant, my darling, I have to admit it was. She flung her arms round me before I could stop her. If you hadn't rushed off like an agitated hen, you would have seen me push her away.'

Abby sighed, remembering the misery and jealousy that the scene had inspired in her. 'I've been a fool, haven't I?' she murmured.

'I've been a bigger one,' he said. 'I should have told you I was in love with you the night I sprang our engagement on you.'

'I don't think I'd have believed you then. I still find it difficult. I'm so different from Vicky Laughton.'

'Thank God for that!' The words were heartfelt. 'Meeting you was the best thing that happened to me, though it took me a little while to realise it. But now I do and ...'

He broke off and a spasm of deep-felt emotion contracted his features.

'If I tell you I will never love another woman the way I love you, you might find that hard to believe, bearing in mind I once entertained the possibility of marrying Vicky. Yet I do want to say it, Abby, because it's true. You've been a revelation to me. Your honesty, your kindness ... Damn it, I've already said that, and I'm fed up with words.'

Once again he started to kiss her, and this time there was no holding back on Abby's part. With all the fervour of her generous nature she responded to him, sinking back on the pillows and pulling him down with her. Their lips fused in a deep penetrating kiss, and the gentle seeking of his hands aroused her to a wondrous awareness that filled her with an urgent need to absorb him. Convulsively she arched her body against his and clasped him close, holding his hands upon her breasts.

'Abby, no!' This time Giles was the one to hold back and, reluctantly but firmly, he pushed himself away from her and stood up. 'When I make love to you for the first time, I want to choose the place and the circumstances. A quiet place,' he added, 'and circumstances where we'll be uninterrupted for a long time.'

'How long?' she whispered.

'A month. A friend of mine has a houseboat in Kashmir which he'd be delighted to loan us—if you can bear the thought of being alone with me for all that length of time?'

'I want to be with you for the rest of my life,' she said simply, and held up her hand to him.

'That, my sweetheart,' he said, holding the tips of her fingers to his lips and nibbling each one gently, 'is a sentiment I completely endorse.'

Take these 4 best-selling novels FREE

ANNE HAMPSON
gates of steel

ANNE MATHER
sweet revenge

VIOLET WINSPEAR
devil in a silver room

JANET DAILEY
no quarter asked